SPE...

CASTERS & CLAWS

NEW YORK TIMES and USA TODAY
BESTSELLING AUTHOR

MILLY TAIDEN

SIGN UP FOR MILLY TAIDEN'S NEWSLETTER FOR LATEST NEWS, GIVEAWAYS, EXCERPTS, AND MORE!
http://eepurl.com/pt9q1

Raven Bishop doesn't need the help of a man, no matter how hot he is. So when an alluring stranger walks into her magic supply shop Gemstones, Raven ignores his advice. He might be a police officer, but she knows she can take care of herself.

Sheriff and wolf shifter Zane Cross has one mission: get the Bishop women away from the order of witch hunters. He doesn't have time to deal with his inner wolf howling that they've finally met their mate. Especially since the woman in question refuses to follow him to safety. Until she's attacked.

In a secluded cabin, far away from the threat of death, the grumpy sheriff and headstrong witch will have to find common ground in order to survive. Can Raven put her pride aside and let love save the day?

This book is a work of fiction. The names, characters, places, and incidents are fictitious or have been used fictitiously, and are not to be construed as real in any way. Any resemblance to persons, living or dead, actual events, locales, or organizations is entirely coincidental.

Published By
Latin Goddess Press, Inc.
Winter Springs, FL 32708
http://millytaiden.com
Spellbound in Salem
Copyright © 2020 by Milly Taiden
Copyright by Latin Goddess Press, Inc.
Edited by: Tina Winograd
Cover: Jacqueline Sweet
All Rights Are Reserved. No part of this book may be used or reproduced in any manner whatsoever without written permission, except in the case of brief quotations embodied in critical articles and reviews.
Property of Milly Taiden
January 2020

❋ Created with Vellum

—For anyone who's ever had their heart broken

There's someone out there that will help put it back together!

CHAPTER ONE

ZANE

The fluorescent light above Zane Cross's desk flickered, giving him a slight headache. A quick glance at his watch confirmed it was going to be a long day. It was barely ten o'clock in the morning.

He'd been up all night at the scene of a robbery, having responded directly to the call instead of staying home. His shift was just starting, and Zane was already beat. Served him right for being a bit of a control freak when it came to patrolling his beloved town of Salem.

His office door swung open, and Axel, the wolf pack's alpha and Zane's closest friend, waltzed in like he owned the place.

"Morning, Sheriff," Axel greeted him, settling on one of the chairs framing his desk.

"It sure is morning," Zane answered. He rubbed his hand across his face, trying to stifle a yawn but failed miserably. The scruff against his palm was a clear sign he hadn't even taken the time to shave in the last few days. The pale blond stubble would have to go as soon as he found a free moment.

Zane couldn't remember the last time he had a decent night's sleep. He knew he needed rest and a couple of days off to restore his energy levels and stock up some patience. He also needed to spend a bit of time in his wolf form, gallivanting through the woods. That would definitely unwind and restore him to his usual high-level professionalism.

A series of odd break-ins had kept him busier than normal. Zane knew all the robberies were connected, but he couldn't garner why or how yet. All he knew was that the same scent lingered in the air at each crime scene, but he hadn't been able to chase down the culprit. They drove away in a vehicle, which took away his ability to track them.

Zane was good, but he wasn't infallible.

"You look like hell," Axel pointed out, no doubt sensing Zane's exhaustion.

"I feel like it, too. As soon as I get the robbery's paperwork settled, I might just take a few days up at my cabin."

If there were no more. If he felt like the town would be safe. If none of his deputies called in sick.

"Good," Axel nodded. "You need it. I won't have my security officer and the town's sheriff collapsing from fatigue."

"I'm fine," he grumbled by way of answer.

Zane was grateful that his friend supported his decision to take over the sheriff's position. Traditionally speaking, that role should have gone to the wolf alpha, but Axel had no desire to police a pack and a whole town. Even if it was tiring work, Zane enjoyed it for the most part. It kept him busy, and he knew he had a knack for protecting and investigating. That was the wolf in him.

"Anything to report?" Axel asked.

The two men had these meetings a few times a month to keep each other abreast of any situations. Zane took care of the human side of town while Axel managed the wolf part of it. If there was any crossover, Zane made sure that the wolves were taken care of on the legal side. It was up to Axel to distribute pack justice.

"Apart from the break-ins, no. There was trouble with a couple of pups two nights ago. There were shifting in the woods behind the primary school, so we had some words."

"Who? I'll make sure to complete a home visit."

Zane flipped open his notepad and rattled off the names of three young wolves. They wouldn't be in any real trouble. No doubt, Axel would stop by and remind them that they weren't to shift where humans could spot them.

"Do you need any noses on these robberies?" Axel asked.

For a few seconds, Zane considered taking his alpha up on the offer, but he thought better of it. This was a town matter, and it'd be dealt with as such.

"Nah, it's all right."

Betty, the officer on desk duty and member of the pack, knocked on the door and popped her head in.

"Hey, Sheriff, Alpha, I hate to bother you, but there is something up front that requires your attention."

"Both of us?" Axel asked, curiosity piqued.

"Sure," Betty answered with a shrug. "There's a young boy here who wants to report a crime, but he says he'll only talk to the sheriff."

"I'll stay put for now," Axel said, taking out his phone.

That was weird. People didn't typically walk in off the street to warn the police. Usually, those things happened via tip lines. Zane pushed back from his desk and followed Betty into the lobby.

The young boy, who on closer inspection was more of a teenager, kept looking over his shoulder. He stood by the high reception desk, shuffling nervously on his feet. His skin was ghostly pale, and his shock of red hair stuck out as if he'd lost a battle with his comb. Something was definitely wrong.

"What's happening, kid?" Zane asked, crossing his arms. His hackles were raised way high.

That was the joy of being a wolf shifter and the sheriff. He could tell when a situation was gearing up to be messed up. And this one was sure to be a dozy, judging by the state the kid was in.

"Well…" The red-haired teen looked over his shoulder again, trying to see through the station's large window.

"You being followed?"

All Zane got was a nod, the teen's eyes still solidly on the door as if he were expecting someone to burst through and drag him away the second he opened his mouth.

"Who by? Are you in danger?"

The headshake the kid gave was hesitant.

Zane needed answers, and signs weren't enough. He'd have a better chance understanding Lassie.

With a sigh, Zane leaned against the counter. Betty shot him a quizzical look. She was also a wolf shifter, and there was no doubt she was also sensing the boy was in some kind of trouble.

"How about you start with your name?" Betty's tone was kind and soft. It was completely at odds with how fierce she was when things got hairy.

The boy's shoulders slumped when Betty spoke to him. He kept his wide, scared eyes on her.

"Levi Griggs," he answered. "I think my dad is going to kill some people." The words came tumbling out in a panic. "You've got to stop him. I don't want to have to hurt anyone."

CHAPTER TWO

ZANE

Levi, the panicked teen, shuffled on his feet, his eyes trained on the ground. His words were heavy and they echoed loudly through the reception area of the sheriff's station.

Zane exchanged another look with his deputy, Betty. No doubt curious about the odd exchange, Axel rounded the corner. Blessed with shifter hearing, the alpha had definitely heard the conversation.

"Why don't you come into my office and chat." Zane motioned for Levi to follow him, but the boy didn't move.

"I don't want to be in trouble," he whispered to the white linoleum floor.

"You won't be," Zane assured him. The sheriff was fairly certain the kid was honest. Levi was a minor, and he was reporting the crime. Judging by the adrenaline and fear rolling off the kid, he hadn't done anything. "Let's talk," Zane said, keeping his tone open and friendly.

Levi eyed the exit, his face a mask of worry and guilt. He shook himself and followed Zane down the long hallway into a small office. On nothing but pure instinct, Zane nodded to Axel, silently asking him to join him.

Axel took his spot on one of the back chairs. Levi hesitated a bit before sitting beside the tall, burly man, but he slouched down with a heavy sigh.

"Okay, Levi. Start at the top," Zane asked, trying to keep his voice calm and steady.

"I… My dad," the kid closed his eyes and took a deep breath. "My family is part of a group of people who want to remove all the witches from Salem."

Axel's eyes shot to Zane, but it was the only outward sign that the two wolves were concerned about Levi's words. If the teen had looked at either man, he would have seen stoic faces.

"It's this whole thing," Levi continued, "my

uncles and a few other men in the town think the descendants of the Salem witches are poisoning the town. They want to kill off all of the people who have the same last name as the people who were hung in 1692. They think that to properly cleanse the town, they have to kill them in the same order as they were executed."

"So, your dad and his buddies want to go out and kill the Bishop women in the town?" Zane asked, keeping his tone calm and leveled. He was even surprised he remembered enough history to recall who had been the first woman to die during the trials that had plagued the town.

"Yeah," Levi confirmed. "There aren't many. Just a few chicks. But my dad wants to kill them today. And he's expecting me to do my share. It's nuts. Witches aren't real. I tried to…" Levi stopped himself, and he looked down to his wringing hands. "I tried to convince them they were just crazy, but that didn't go over too well."

"So when is this attack happening?" Zane pressed.

"Sometime this morning. I guess as soon as I get back to my dad's place. He doesn't know I snuck out, and I don't know how I'm going to explain this when I slink back into the house."

"Oh, you're not going anywhere," Zane said. "How old are you, Levi?"

"I'm seventeen," the kid answered.

"Right. So you're a minor. In good conscience, I can't let you go out there when your dad might decide to do something dangerous. I'll set you up in one of the interrogation rooms with Officer Betty Armstrong. You can tell her everything you feel comfortable. We'll make sure your pops doesn't do anything rash."

"I don't want him arrested, but…" Levi was clearly torn about the hard choice he had made.

Zane could only admire the kid for being so strong, for having such a good moral compass.

"You said your father and the others were targeting a specific family. The Bishop women, is that right?"

"Yeah. There's only four of them left in town, and they're youngish. Like, they could be moms, maybe." Levi shivered as he spoke those last words, making Zane feel for the kid.

It couldn't have been easy for Levi to come here and explain all of this to the authorities. It was the right thing to do, of course.

"How do you know there are only a few

Bishops left in Salem?" Axel asked. He stole the question out of Zane's mouth.

"The basement at the house kind of became a war room. There's a list of all the people who are descendants from the Salem witches. They're all the targets that the Order of Salem wants to take out."

"Say that name again," Axel demanded, using his alpha tone on the poor trembling kid.

"The Order of Salem," Levi repeated.

Zane and Axel exchanged a wary look. It sounded vaguely familiar to Zane, but judging by the frown on Axel's face, the pack alpha knew something. As leader of the wolves, Axel knew a lot more of Salem's history, especially everything that was linked to the supernatural.

"This is at your house?" Zane watched the kid nod and passed him a notepad and a pen. "Can you jot down your address, bud? And a list of all the people who are in the Order of Salem, if you can remember any."

The teen's hands trembled as he wrote down his home address. Tears began to line his eyes. "I don't want anyone to get hurt," he sniffled.

"You're doing the right thing," Zane assured him. "The right thing isn't always easy, but it's worth it. We'll look into this. It could be that your dad is just going to try and scare them away. Chase them out of town."

Levi shook his head. "He has a bunch of guns. He means business. They all do."

"That's all right. That's why my officers are here. To serve and protect. Now, let's get you to give all of the information you can while we track down the Bishop women to keep them safe."

As both a wolf and a sheriff, defending his town and its inhabitants was all that mattered to Zane.

CHAPTER THREE

ZANE

As Zane led a shaken Levi to one of the small interrogation rooms, he tried to help the kid stay calm. It wasn't easy. Levi was having all sorts of emotions, most of which played out on his young, pale face. To help with the shock, Zane gave him a bottle of water.

"You need to drink this, okay?" Zane said. "It'll help settle your nerves. Agent Armstrong will be with you in a couple of minutes. Hang tight, bud."

With Axel on his heels, Zane went into the reception area to give Betty a brief rundown of what was happening.

"You stay here and get as much information as you can out of him. He's a minor, so don't go in there without one of the social workers. Call them and let them know the situation. They'll put a rush on it. We'll go to the kid's place. I want to make sure this has no ties to any pack enemies before I proceed strictly with mortal, human law. If anything happens here, let me know."

Zane pulled another of his officers, tasking him with running Levi's father through the system, as well as the list of names Levi had given him.

With as many things taken care of at the station as possible, Zane knew he had to make his way to the Griggs house to intercept the attack. He hopped into his sheriff's truck while Axel took his own vehicle. It was always better to have two cars in case things went sideways fast, especially when supernatural things were at play.

Levi couldn't possibly know witches were real.

They were, though Zane had never had any real run-ins with them. They were a more insular community who took care of their own, very similar to the wolf pack. If humans were hunting witches, that toed the line between what he could do as a sheriff and what Axel could do as pack alpha.

This was where their solid teamwork was a

bonus. They could cover all of the bases, keeping most of Salem safe.

The Griggs family home had seen better days. The siding was chipped in a few places, the roof needed replacing, and the shutters were falling off their hinges.

Zane tapped on the door, announcing police presence.

"Did you hear that?" he said, feigning to hear someone in distress in the house.

"Sure did," Axel nodded that he was ready.

With a good kick to the door, Zane burst into the house, gun drawn. The first floor of the house was clear, and they made their way to the basement.

The dark wood paneling of the walls was nearly covered in papers and notes. None of it looked good. It made the hair at the back of Zane's neck stand on edge.

"This is some fucked up shit." Axel whistled through his teeth, taking in what could only be called a kill list etched on one of the walls.

Zane pointed to the Bishop line that had a large one written in red beside it. "There are four Bishop women still living in Salem," he said, reading over the list. "We need to warn them and get them the hell away from here while we put this to rest."

"What's the plan, Sheriff?" Axel asked.

It was always a little odd when his alpha deferred to him, but Zane appreciated that his leader trusted his judgment enough to make these calls. It was why he was sheriff, after all. Zane knew one of his strengths was analyzing a situation to formulate the best course of action. In this case, whatever he chose to do, he needed to do it fast since Levi's dad wasn't in the house. That could only mean the man was preparing for his attack on the Bishops.

"You take one of the ladies, I'll get another," Zane pointed to two of the names. "I think we should ask some of the others to keep an eye on pack business while we deal with this."

"I agree," Axel nodded. "I am not letting any sort of anti-paranormal vigilante hunt near my pack."

"Right," Zane said. "We should get Blaze and Jett in on this. Those in the next town over could also be affected if the Order of Salem decides to chase down the witches beyond the city limits."

"That's a valid point."

Axel grabbed his phone and called Blaze

Spinner and Jett Arrowood, the wolf alpha and his enforcer, who had lands in the next town over. As Axel spoke to the other alpha, Zane stood back and stared at the wall.

If anything, it was pretty fucking clear the Order of Salem meant business. They wanted to kill witches, and they didn't necessarily care to prove if these people were supernatural or not.

It seemed to Zane there was a bunch of lunatics who wanted to kill but were hiding behind a mask of righteousness. It made him sick. The majority of the targets were women who had done nothing. Innocents who just so happen to have last names tied to the executed witches.

"Blaze and Jett are heading out to take these two," Axel pointed to two names, Astra and Selene. "They live on the edge of town, so those are the most likely to splash into their territory."

"I'll take the store, you take the house. Whoever gets to Raven and Cerise first, let's keep in touch. But really, we should keep them all separate with the next family, the Goods, on the list under surveillance."

There was a large number two by the Good family tree, indicating they were to be the next targets once the Bishops were taken care of. "If the Order of Salem is spread out, and they can't find the first victims, they might not act right away. We will have time to formulate a plan."

"How do you want to play this, Sheriff?" Axel asked. "Do we follow the law?"

"I think we need to for now. They haven't hurt any wolves or any other living person. Let's just get the Bishops out of Salem while we track the Order down."

Zane looked around the room once more. He wished he could garner how many members were in the Order of Salem and how many weapons they had. It would also have been useful to find some kind of manifesto to understand why these people wanted to eradicate witches. Zane found that knowing the why usually made an investigation much easier. It also gave him ideas on how to deal with the guilty parties.

He'd deal with that later. First, he needed to find the Bishop women and save them.

CHAPTER FOUR

RAVEN

Raven walked down the center aisle of her small, yet filled, new age store. Gemstones were her pride and joy. She'd built a reputable and respected business with her sister. The store had been open for nearly ten years, but Raven still felt a zing of pride when she walked through the space filled with crystals, books, herbs, and various other witch paraphernalia.

Her wooden clipboard was tucked under her arm as she surveyed the shelves. This was one of her favorite parts of the job. Doing inventory might be boring and tedious for some, but Raven found it soothing. More than that, it gave her the store's pulse. She knew exactly what was selling, what hadn't moved in a little while. It helped her feel connected to the store and to her customers.

Oh, crap.

Raven jotted down that they were almost out of lavender candles and peppermint scrub. It would definitely need to be a rush order to make sure the good people of Salem had all of the relaxing and invigorating equipment they needed to get through their days.

As she made the note, she continued her progress down the aisle. The old wooden floor creaked under her feet, but it was a comforting sound. Like the history of the building was protecting her and her business. The weathered dark timber had been restored and was in great condition, but Raven could still feel the past thrumming through it.

Her eyes snapped forward at sudden movement, and Raven clamped her jaw in annoyance.

"Stop right there," Raven said, using her most authoritative voice, pointing to the shoplifter.

The redhead was none other than her cousin Astra. Her family member had a proclivity for pilfering a few items here and there. Raven didn't mind so much, but she had told her cousin time and time again that it was bad for business.

Astra turned to face Raven with a big grin on her face. She didn't actually stop what she was doing, though, the silver gleam of the necklace's chain sparkling in her hand.

"Put that back, Astra," Raven demanded again. "You so did not pay for that."

"Oh, come on," Astra whined. "You know I need the boost the rose quartz gives me. It totally counteracts the negativity Mrs. Gellar brings in during her sessions. You're basically doing a public service by giving me this. That's a tax write-off."

It wasn't. Raven took a few more steps, intent on taking the necklace from Astra. She was too late. Her cousin closed the clasp of the necklace around her neck and spun it around so that the small pink stone laid against her throat. Raven sighed and rolled her eyes to the heavens.

"How are Cerise and I suppose to make any sort of profit if you're always stealing our shit?"

Astra blew her a kiss, dramatically smacking her lips together.

"I gave you a soul-cleansing last week," Astra explained. "I didn't charge you, so think of this as my payment."

"Hey, now. You insisted on doing that. As

practice. You can't charge me retroactively because you like the new pieces we have in stock. Besides, I know for a fact you already have a rose quartz necklace. You took it from that very display case last month."

"Yes," Astra said, walking toward the exit. "Because that was the last time Mrs. Gellar was coming in from an appointment. I swear she is an energy vampire."

"You know you could just buy the necklace," Raven called out. "Or I swear, I'll let it slip to my mother that you're playing the magpie."

Astra stopped dead in her tracks and turned back to face Raven. Her eyes were narrowed, her mouth opened in surprise. Raven gave her a triumphant look. Astra was more of a sister than a cousin, and her threat had been nothing more than a good old sibling trick.

"You wouldn't," Astra gasped.

"I sure would," Raven smirked. "My mother called yesterday so I am expecting another call this afternoon. I just have to let it slip that you took a necklace, and next thing you know, Auntie Edith will be calling you so fast…"

Inhaling deeply, Astra shook her head. "You're a traitor, Raven. You wouldn't."

"Wouldn't I? Payback for stealing the necklace and for telling your mom about Arthur."

Astra's face paled. "You know I didn't mean to let it slip that you'd dumped him." Astra dug a ten-dollar bill out of her pocket and slammed it onto the small counter at the very front where the cash register sat.

"It's better to pay for it, anyway," Raven pointed out. "You wouldn't want to mess with the energies by having a stolen crystal protecting you."

"Ugh. You're right. So how are our dear parents, anyway?" Astra asked.

This was the way of the Bishop women. Fighting one second, perfectly harmonious the next. Some said it was because they were temperamental women, but the Bishops knew the truth. It's because they were witches.

"Well," Raven shrugged, "our mothers seem to be enjoying themselves on the cruise. But apparently, at the last port, both of our dads staged a protest. I quote, the damned boat was moving too much."

"Ah, I told them that being a water witch didn't necessarily mean they'd be comfortable on a moving ship. Fuck!" Astra shouted, her eyes on the small clock above the register. "I'll be late for Mrs. Gellar. Don't tell my mom. Bye." She took the ten-dollar bill back and slid it into her pocket.

Raven didn't even try to stop her cousin. She was already halfway out the door anyway. Grumbling to herself about her eccentric family member, Raven went back into the store's aisles to continue the inventory.

But a few short moments passed when the small bell over the door dinged, signaling a new patron. Raven hoped it wasn't Astra who'd come back for more freebies. She ducked her head around the high shelf and plastered on her best retail smile.

"Be with you in just a second."

The man who was standing there in the brown sheriff's uniform made Raven's heart speed up. His green eyes caught her own, and Raven forgot what she had been doing but two seconds before. If she didn't know any better, Raven would have sworn that the stranger was undressing her with his eyes. And all he could see was her scooped-neck pink top and her head of black hair.

Raven sent out a silent thank you to the universe that she had actually taken care to wrangle her messy curls into straight, smooth tresses that morning. She couldn't help but be interested in the attractive man. *No*, her heart cried. *No more dudes. You promised no more after Arthur.* Raven ignored her still shattered heart. She couldn't very well ignore a potential customer.

She dropped her clipboard on the shelf and made her way to him.

As she did, she let her eyes roam over him. He was a beast. Easily a foot taller than her five-foot-four frame. He was wide in the shoulders and narrowed down at the waist. The ugly brown pants and tan-colored shirt shouldn't, logically, look good on anyone. But she was definitely affected by the uniform. Or rather, the man draped in it. His muscular forearms were clearly on display, the hem of the shirt working around his biceps. His blond hair was swooped back as if he'd been running his hands through the strands continuously.

"Raven Bishop?" the man asked. Oh, sweet lord. His voice was deep and clear. The way he'd said her name gave her chills.

"Yes?" she asked. She'd never admit to anyone, but she was hoping someone had sent her a stripper-gram as a joke. That would be something her cousins would do to mess with her. No sheriff had any right being this hot. Not with a jaw that square and full lips hidden behind a bit of pale blond scruff.

"I'm Sheriff Cross. I've got a matter of some urgency I need to discuss with you."

Raven's heart started to beat faster, but not because Sheriff Cross was drop-dead gorgeous. Rather, because she'd realized that an actual officer of the law was standing in her store, asking to speak with her.

Could she be arrested for letting Astra take a few things from inventory?

What? No. That made no sense. Raven swallowed against her dry throat.

"Sure. Okay," she managed to say.

"I need to take you to a safe location." He gestured toward the door like she would just follow him out of the store and into his cruiser.

"What? I don't think so." Her face flushed, and she crossed her arms. "I'm going to have to ask to see your badge."

Her mama hadn't raised any fools. She knew a few serial killers pretended to be cops and made away with unsuspecting women. Raven wasn't about to trust a pretty face and a uniform. He was too good-looking to be deserving of her trust. *Yup,* her poor heart agreed. *We don't trust sexy men anymore.*

Sheriff Cross—if that was even his name—pulled out his badge and held it out for her to see. Raven took the piece of identification in her hands and flipped it every which way until she was positive it was real.

"You're going to explain to me why I need to go anywhere with you," she said, handing him back his badge.

"You're in danger. I can't give you more details than that. Not here. Not now. It's not safe."

"I'm sorry, am I supposed to understand what you're saying right now?" Her sudden attraction to Sheriff Cross was quickly ebbing away.

He closed the distance between them, coming to stand so close to her, she could see the different shades of blond in his hair and facial hair. So close, she could smell the faint hint of cologne.

"I don't mean to sound dramatic, Ms. Bishop," he said, "but you need to come with me if you want to live."

CHAPTER FIVE

RAVEN

ome with me if you want to live.

Sheriff Cross's words reverberated through the small store and Raven couldn't help it.

She began to laugh.

And not a dainty little giggle she could easily recover from. Oh, no.

This was a deep belly laughed that left her snorting every time she tried to kill the laughter. Tears sprang up in her eyes, and she dabbed at them, hoping her mascara wasn't a running mess.

Sheriff Cross looked at her, green eyes wide and mouth wide open in shock and confusion. Raven held out a finger to him, gesturing that she needed a second—or sixty—to compose herself.

"Sorry," she managed to say after a few more spurts of laughter. "You have to know how silly that sounded. You took that from an action movie, you can't blame me for laughing so hard. It was cheesy in the movie, but in real life, it's just..." She gulped around the next wave of laughter threatening to bubble out of her.

"Right, well, that doesn't change the fact we need to go. You are in danger."

"Can you clarify this danger?" Raven asked, her breath still choppy from all of the laughing. God, he was hot. She had to make sure to look away. She definitely didn't need to notice how square his jaw was.

The last square jaw she'd been interested in had taken her heart, stomped on it, stabbed it with a poisonous dagger, and then set it on fire just for good measure.

"I'd rather we wait until we were far away from here. It's for your own security. This store isn't safe. The Order of Salem is after you and your kin."

"The what, now? Is that the people who threw holy water on me at the grocery store last week? I didn't press charges. I just got a little bit wet. It's fine."

"No, Ms. Bishop." The sheriff looked around and sighed, looking completely resigned. "I know you're a witch. A descendant from Salem's own Bridget Bishop who was killed in 1692. There is a group of people, calling themselves the Order of Salem, and their mandate, their entire reason for existing, is to completely destroy all of the Salem witch bloodlines. From what we've learned, your family is the first to be targeted because your ancestor was the first to be executed. They know, or in the very least, suspect you're witches."

"You're high on something, mister," Raven said, rolling her eyes. "There is no such thing as witches."

The sheriff shook his head. "We both know that's not true. I know my fair share about the paranormal world. It's okay."

Raven watched him intently. If the sheriff knew about the magic in her bloodline, was it possible that others had also figured it out?

"I assure you, Ms. Bishop. I know you're a witch, just like the rest of your family. This is important. Please, let's not pretend that supernatural don't exist."

Well, shit. There was no denying it since he was so adamant about it.

"Fine," Raven sighed. "So what if I am? There is no way that anyone knows we're real witches."

Her words didn't match the way her eyes were darting to the door or how her heart rate had seriously increased in the last few seconds. Raven might say she wasn't worried, but she was lying. She knew that some people still held out a weird sort of hope that witches were real and could be killed. Her kind had always been chased down, and that wasn't about to change.

Though she was fairly surprised this one particular threat had made its way up to the town's sheriff, there was no way she was going to be scared or run out of town because of it. Her ancestors had been through that, but she wouldn't bend or fold. She was a Bishop, and damn proud of it. If anyone thought attacking her was a good idea, Raven would use her magic to protect herself and her people. It was that simple.

That was something the sexy sheriff couldn't possibly understand. Sure, he was a man of the law who had taken an oath to serve and protect the people of the town. But there was no way he could understand the stress that came from knowing that your family members had been prosecuted and killed merely for being different.

Raven was happy to be a witch, and she wouldn't let anyone make her feel like it was bad to be who she was, to be born with special gifts. Not anymore, anyway. She'd drank that Kool-Aid and it hadn't been good

It wasn't like this was the first threat she had faced. When she'd been a small child, a few women had approached her, her twin, and cousins in the park, and they'd been particularly nasty. They'd also been from an organization that wanted to remove all traces of Salem's witches from existence. It hadn't gone anywhere, though, because Raven's mom and aunt had intervened pretty quickly.

And then there was Arthur and his less than ideal reaction to her witchiness.

Because fucking a series of women behind her back had only happened after she'd confessed she was a witch. That's what her asshole ex had said. Not that Raven believed him for five seconds. But the fact that Arthur had used her lineage as the reason for his cheating had stung. Cut. Burned.

"Others definitely know about the existence of real witches."

She shook her head at him, but he went on, not giving her a chance to interrupt.

"I know this is a lot to take in," he said, "but you really are a target."

"Well," Raven shot back, crossing her arms, "if I'm a target, then so are my sister and my cousins. Why didn't you go to them?" Raven didn't believe they would have been likelier to believe him.

"I have people going to each Bishop woman within the city limits. Your parents moved away, correct?"

"Yes, my parents and aunt and uncle live in sunny California now. They are also off on a cruise, so they're safe from whatever Order is after us. So am I, by the way."

Sheriff Cross's eyebrows shot up into his hairline. "You really don't believe me that you're being threatened."

"Hmm, no. I don't think this is a real thing. We've been threatened before. Some holy water was thrown. I have had some vandalism to the store a few times, but nothing on my life. People aren't as quick to kill witches as they were in the seventeenth century."

"Oh?" It was his turn to cross his arms then. "Do you do much research on the murder rate?"

"Look, you're here. You've warned me. Your officers have warned my sister and my cousins. That's fine. We'll take care of our own."

"You can't stay in Salem, Ms. Bishop. These people have guns and a kill list. This is very real."

"I can't stay in Salem? Look around," she gestured to the store. "This is where my business is. This is my home. I won't be run out. I need a hell of a lot more than a threat to make me go." Hell, her break-up with Arthur hadn't sent her packing. And neither would this half-baked threat.

"Am I going to have to put you under arrest to get you to come with me?" Sheriff Cross asked.

More laughter bubbled out of Raven.

"We both know you can't do that. You came to warn me. I've been officially told about the threat. Now, if you could just go, I have a business to run. And I need to call my sister to make sure she's okay and not off somewhere with one of your men."

"Let me ask you this, Ms. Bishop," Sheriff Cross took a few more steps toward her. "If the Order of Salem were to walk into the store right now, would you do magic to defend yourself?"

"Of course," Raven answered without hesitating.

"And do you think your magic can save you from a bullet? Because the man in charge of the Order has a son. He's the one who told us about the attack, and he mentioned that his father had multiple weapons and quite a few allies. All armed."

Raven faltered. Her bravado might be misplaced. She knew she couldn't deal with this alone. There was strength in numbers.

What she needed to do was call Cerise and come up with a plan to deal with this. There was no way she was involving the mortal cops in witch business. Even if the threat came from humans. As per usual.

Raven didn't need the sexy sheriff. She could take care of her own. She'd been doing it all her life and the one time she'd trusted a man to be there for her, he'd disappointed her so hard she still hurt from it. No, Raven could and would handle whatever was coming without needing the sheriff.

CHAPTER SIX

ZANE

Raven Bishop stood before him, arms crossed, and delicate chin turned up. Zane could tell she wasn't going to come with him easily. He was already standing close to her, closer than he probably should be, but he couldn't help himself.

Even in the small store jammed-packed full of all kinds of things he had never seen before, his senses were flooded by smells, but it didn't matter.

Not really.

Because deep inside himself, Zane could feel his wolf pacing impatiently, growling, and demanding to be let out to sniff the beauty standing in front of them.

Zane couldn't swat the animal away.

He knew there was nothing to do about the canine's reaction.

Raven Bishop, witch and murder-plot victim, was his mate.

She was his. His to care for, his to protect.

His hands balled up into fists at his side. What a pain in the ass. He didn't have time to be distracted by his shifter instincts. He had a town to protect and an insane order of witch hunters to thwart. None of that was conducive to losing his head—both of them—to the raven-haired beauty.

Well, shit. He was even waxing poetic in his head, comparing her hair to the bird whose feathers her locks matched perfectly. It even went with her name.

Zane had had every intention of walking into the store to have a calm conversation with Raven and Cerise Bishop about the danger they were in. He had planned on piling them in his truck to lead them to a nearby cabin where they would be safe for the foreseeable future while he dealt with the Order of Salem with his pack and his deputies.

The fact that Raven was his mate changed everything.

Zane was not letting her out of his sight.

Whether it was convenient or not, Raven was his to protect.

He took stock of what he knew. Firstly, Zane had the distinct impression that convincing Raven that she needed to come with him would be difficult. Secondly, he knew that with his mate sense blaring in his head as his wolf howled for Raven, there was no way he could leave her side. His wolf would tear at his skin if he even tried to leave the woman in someone else's care.

"What does the Order of Salem know about the supernatural, anyway? What do you know about it? I'll call my sister and get this all squared away."

The thought of Raven facing down an angry armed mob with her sister terrified him.

Taking a deep breath, Zane made the decision to be as honest as possible with Raven. There was no way around it. If he didn't tell her now, it would only make things more awkward later when he had to tell her. When he seduced her. Because he would.

Zane searched his brain for a frame of reference, but he came up short. He'd never had to tell a woman he had to protect her since she was his fated mate. Perhaps this is what Raven needed to put her trust in him completely.

"Miss Bishop, I have to be honest with you before we go any further." Raven crossed her arms again, pursing her lips. "I'm a shifter," he blurted out, "and my wolf is adamant that you're my mate. Though that complicates the current situation, I assure you I will remain completely professional. I promise that I will put those feelings aside until this situation is resolved."

Zane could hear Raven's heart thundering in his own ears, and he wondered what had made her pulse increase. She'd been fairly calm until he mentioned she was his mate.

"Have you lost your noodles?" Raven's hazel eyes were all but popping out of her beautiful face. "You can't just walk up to a woman and be like, hey, so these people are out to kill you. Oh, and I'm your mate but have no fear, I will be professional and won't chase you until you're safe. Who taught you how to talk to women?"

He couldn't help but be confused by her reaction.

Zane knew it was less than ideal for him to be mated to her, but it was better he be upfront about it. He hadn't expected Raven to be angry about it. Overwhelmed? Sure. But not flat out upset.

"I only mention it because I don't want to be an issue between us."

"An issue?" Raven gasped. "Sheriff Cross…"

"Zane," he interrupted her, suddenly longing to hear her say his name. "Please, call me Zane."

"Fine," she sighed. "Zane, you can't just expect me to follow you around and take your orders because you say I'm your fated mate. It doesn't work like that. This is the twenty-first century. I'm not just going to take your word for it and fawn all over you."

He took in her words. He had to admit they made sense. Now he just had to figure out how to backpedal and get Raven to agree to go into hiding with him.

Fuck. Why had he been honest about the mate thing?

Right.

Pure instincts. He had to tell her. His wolf commanded it. Besides, he had to be honest with her. It would make it a hell of a lot easier for him when this was all done. If Raven already knew he was attached to her, it would be easier for her to trust him.

"I'm not asking you to follow me blindly. I am warning you that there is a threat against your life and that as a police officer and a wolf, I am here to protect you. I won't let you face this alone. Especially not since we don't know how dangerous these people are."

"Correction," Raven interjected. "They don't know how dangerous I am."

Zane didn't know whether he wanted to kiss her or spank her for being so sure of herself. She was brave, and the cop in him admired her for it. But that courage was also foolish, and that made the wolf in him get all kinds of annoyed.

"Would you be able to hurt someone?" he asked. Raven deflated.

There was the crux of it all.

Raven wanted to deal with this threat with her family, but when the Order of Salem came, there was no telling how Raven would react. Would she defend herself, or would she falter, scared of hurting another human being?

His money was on the latter.

"What can I do to convince you to come with me?" he asked her.

Zane knew he must be running out of time. Soon, the Order of Salem would drive up to the store, and they'd no doubt try to complete their mission.

"Let me think on that," Raven answered, her gaze on his mouth. "I'll let you know if and when I decide you're correct."

She turned on her heels and disappeared down the aisle. Zane watched her go but didn't leave. He crossed his arms and leaned against the small counter. If she wasn't going to go with him, he'd wait.

He'd be there when the Order appeared, and then, Raven would see that she needed him.

CHAPTER SEVEN

RAVEN

"You're still here?" she asked with a grin, rounding the corner of one of the aisles to see Zane.

In truth, Raven had known he hadn't left. The little bell over the door hadn't tolled. She knew the sheriff was still in her store, waiting to prove a point.

Ha.

He'd so totally lose face when the Order of Salem never showed. Quacks like that were unreliable.

"I told you I would protect you," Zane answered.

The man looked about as hot as he could, leaning on her counter. He was flipping through a book called *Hexes and Everyday Curses* as if it were the morning paper. Raven knew the book held some pretty gross hexes, but Zane didn't seem fazed by it at all.

Arthur had only seen a pocket-sized book about everyday spells, and he'd blanched before exploding in a huge tantrum about magic. Was that the time he'd accused her of putting a love spell on him? No. That was another time. Fuck, Raven had stayed with that asshole far too long.

Shaking her head against thoughts of Arthur, Raven brought herself back to Sheriff Hot Stuff.

A quick look at the clock told her that he'd been in the store for over fifteen minutes, just looking through a spell book. Didn't he have a job to do? A town to protect? She opened her mouth to ask him that very question, but her words died.

From the storefront window, Raven watched an old rusty black car whip into the parking lot and come to a sudden and jerky stop. The few seconds made the entire air still around her. All of her witch instincts screamed that this wasn't good.

Three men got out of the car. Each of them held a gun.

"Fucking fuck," Raven gasped. She turned to face Zane already taking out his own weapon.

"You were right." She was completely bemused by the fact that Zane's warning was coming to fruition.

"Get behind me," he ordered, his hand going around her waist as he pulled her behind him.

"I've got this," she murmured.

Raven rubbed her hands together, and she racked her brain for the defensive spells she knew. There wasn't much she could do about their guns. She was an air witch, which meant she might be able to deflect their bullets. There was no way she could mess with the mechanics of the gun. She'd need Astra's fire power for that.

"Raven, this isn't the time. Get back, and let me arrest these guys."

Oh.

Arrest them.

Right.

That was a good solid plan. What the fuck was wrong with her? She knew she shouldn't debate in the face of danger, but something about this sheriff made her want to dig her heels in. Raven wanted the Order of Salem to be dealt with, but she supposed that having the sheriff there, ready to book them into county jail, was comforting.

Zane walked out of the store, gun drawn.

"Weapons down and hands up, boys." His deep voice was pure business.

Raven knew if she was on the receiving end of such a commanding tone, she would have dropped her weapons. And maybe even her underwear, but that was beside the point.

"Sheriff Cross," the leader of the little crew said, "this business doesn't concern you. There are powers at work in this town you can't protect us from."

"Oh?" Zane infused just enough confusion in his tone to be caught between condescending and understanding. "What forces are those?"

"We can handle this, Sheriff. Please step away from the store. We've done dealt with the shifters because they've been around forever and you don't go around using magic trying to hypnotize people into doing whatever you want. So move out of the way and we'll handle her."

From her vantage point, Raven couldn't tell if the men were rattled by the sheriff's presence at her store. It didn't seem to faze them in the least.

"Can't let you harm anyone," Zane said, cool and calm.

"This isn't a person. It's a witch."

"Still," Zane shrugged like he didn't have three armed assailants in front of him.

It was kind of dangerous. And a little bit sexy. Raven didn't know where the thought came from, but it irked her. She shouldn't be looking at the sheriff, being accosted by three lunatics, like he was the hottest thing around. So what if he had that big sexy body that was clearly full of muscles. And a face she could see herself licking all over.

That was just wrong.

Raven had never been a badge bunny, and she wasn't about to start now. Even if Zane had said she was his mate.

That didn't mean she needed to be with him.

Focus, Raven.

She needed to find a way to help Zane, but how? She couldn't just walk out of Gemstones and be all, hey, boys, I'm here. She'd be killed for sure. And she was way too young to die. There was a lot of things she still wanted to do.

Grow her store, maybe add some new-age classes to the business. If she was lucky enough, she could even find her own place. She'd had to move with her twin after breaking up with Arthur. Raven wanted a cute little house on the edge of town. Maybe one with a large garden where she could grow herbs for her spells.

And maybe, one day, far, far, fucking far into the future, she could find a nice man to settle down with, have a bunch of orgasms and have cute little witch babies.

Not wolf babies. Nope. What would that even look like?

Raven shook her head. So not the time to be thinking about this. *Yeah,* her heart griped, *you promised no more dudes.* That's right. No more men. Even if she really wanted to find out what a night with the sheriff might be like. Would he use his cuffs? She cleared her throat. She did not need to get turned on at that moment. Besides, she needed to focus on what she could do.

She was a Bishop. A powerful witch from a long line of witches. She could help. She would help. There was no way she was going to stand by while the big, bad wolf huffed and puffed the bad guys away.

With quick, steady steps, Raven made her way to the back of the store and exited, using the service entrance used for deliveries. She snuck up the alley that divided her store and the health food store next door. Every step took her closer to the parking lot where the standoff was happening.

Raven peeked around the corner to see the three members of the Order of Salem and Zane were still at a standstill. Taking in the distance between her and the men and making sure she didn't knock Zane down, Raven muttered a spell under her breath.

It didn't take long for the magic to work. The air in the alleyway swirled like it had been shaken by a huge invisible hand. It picked up speed, making her hair whip in her face. The temperature had dropped significantly. With shaking hands, she motioned through the air, sending it to the three attackers. The wind in the alley pushed at her legs in a powerful gale. She definitely hadn't expected to get caught up in the magic wind. The force of the push made Raven stumble out of the alleyway.

She was no longer hidden behind the brick wall, but fully in the crazy dudes' line of sight.

Oops.

Her offensive magic clearly needed a bit of work. Raven truly thought that because her defensive magic and household spells were the best, she could easily get a handle on other parts of magic.

Clearly not.

A bullet cracked against the brick wall beside her head.

"Holy shit!" Raven shouted, ducking for cover.

Two inches to the left, and she would have been dead.

Fuck. Fuck. Fuck.

Why had that wind knocked her down instead of the insane men trying to harm her? The magic hadn't even reached them.

Officer McHot was right. The Order of Salem were after her. And they definitely meant business. Raven hoped that Cerise and her cousins were safe. Maybe if the order was at her door, it meant the others weren't under attack.

That was fine by Raven. Better her than the others.

Raven army crawled to her car. It was right there, but a few feet away from her. The little red vehicle would offer very little protection from bullets, but it was better than nothing. She needed cover to be able to work her magic. If it actually worked this time. Maybe she had said the words wrong.

With as much speed as she could muster, she

spoke an incantation to protect herself from harm. As she inched toward the car, a few more shots rang out, missing her thanks to her spell. That was comforting. At least her defensive magic was working properly.

With her back against the car, she peeked a look toward Zanc.

He wasn't standing there anymore.

What she did see was a pile of brown and beige clothes on the ground and a gray wolf jumping through the air, jowl wide open and aiming for the jugular of one of the three men.

He had mentioned he was a wolf shifter, but that didn't make this situation any more surreal.

You do magic, and you're surprised that a man can transform into a wolf?

Well, at least that made some sort of sense. She bent the rules of air and made it her bitch. Zane had completely changed the physiology of his body from man to beast.

Shaking her head, she remembered she had to focus. What spell could stop a bullet in its tracks when they were so far away? That was way beyond the scope of the magic she knew offhand. Raven would have to get creative. Even if her head felt woozy and the world was starting to tilt a bit. What was happening?

From her hiding spot, she twirled her fingers through the air until she could feel a solid ball of air in her hands. The weight of it was similar to that of a baseball, and nearly the same size. With all her strength, she threw the airball at the man aiming a gun at Zane's wolf shape.

Her pitch was weak, and it barely thunked the guy on the head. He roared and looked around, furious.

"Come out and face me, you wicked witch!" he screamed.

Wicked witch? Oh, hell, no!

He wanted wicked, he'd get it.

CHAPTER EIGHT

RAVEN

With her ass on the cold pavement and an eye on the three men who were trying to get the best of Wolf Zane, Raven twirled her hands, trying to capture as much air as she could.

This time, her airball had to be bigger and pack more of a punch when it hit the lunatics. No one assumed she was evil. No one attacked her without knowing her. No one went after her family.

Raven would show them.

The airball was about the size of a football and weighed about five pounds. It was the best she could do since she still had to throw the damn thing at the bad guys.

Gathering her courage, Raven stood and launched the airball. A loud grunt ripped out of her as she poured her energy into the throw. Her head felt heavy, and she began to pant as if she were running a full marathon. Seriously, what the fuck was that all about?

This time, the airball caught one of the guys straight in the chest. He stumbled back and fell onto his back with a loud scream. It must have hurt.

Raven took no pleasure in knowing she had hurt another human, but he had attacked first. More than that, he was trying to hurt her, her sister, her cousins, and Zane. An officer. That was a federal crime or something. These men were obviously out of touch with reality.

Intent on helping Zane, who had bitten through the leader's leg and was circling the last man standing, Raven did her thing.

The air wasn't responsive. All she could collect was a tablespoon. Her fingers trembled, and her arms felt like jelly. She'd heard of being magically depleted, but she had never felt it before.

It wasn't pleasant.

And she'd only thrown two attacks. Sure, that last one had been a biggy, and the man was still lying on the ground from the force, but Raven was furious she couldn't do anything more. She had to sit back and watch as Zane chomped at the last assailant's leg. The sheriff wasn't aiming to kill these men, merely to incapacitate them. No doubt this was because it would be hard to explain a wolf attacking three grown, armed men to his superiors.

Raven looked around, searching for some kind of weapon, anything that could help Zane.

She couldn't get into her car and use that as a weapon, she'd left her purse and keys in the store. Oh! But Zane must have had his keys in his clothes. Raven crab-walked to the pile of torn brown uniform. His gun and badge where on top of his clothes. She picked up his gun and bad and rifled through his pockets. The key fob in her hand felt like a victory. With his gun and badge on hand, she unlocked the truck and ran to it.

As soon as she closed the door, she cranked the engine and threw the passenger door wide open. If anything, Wolf Zane could hop in, and they could regroup. It was a good plan. Raven was proud of it.

"Zane!" she shouted at him, gesturing from him to jump in.

The wolf shook his head and went back to snarling at the men. It was a good intimidation tactic, but unless Zane had learned how to handcuff perpetrators while in wolf shape, there was no way they were getting the upper hand.

The loud sound of screeching tires had Raven's head whipping around.

An SUV barreled down the street. Judging by the way the vehicle was being driven, Raven knew it had to be more Order of Salem members.

"Get in the truck!" she yelled to the sheriff.

Zane saw the car from which three men and a woman got out and he ran toward her. With an impressive bounce, he landed on the passenger seat and growled at her.

Taking it as a sign to go, Raven put the pedal to the metal and drove away. One of the new attackers aimed a gun at the truck. The bullet crashed into the rear window.

"Thank fuck for bulletproof glass," Raven said after shrieking for only a second. Or two.

The wolf beside her started to change and morph, fur disappearing into flesh and elongating until the gray pelt was replaced by smooth, golden skin with the lightest dusting of blond hair.

It was a fascinating transformation. Raven couldn't look away.

But then she had to, to drive, feeling her skin flush and heat to a thousand degrees.

"Um…" she stammered awkwardly. "Just in case you didn't remember, you're not wearing any clothes."

Raven knew her face was completely red. The skin burned with the effort it took not to look down at his dick. Again.

Because she had definitely seen it.

She kept her gaze up and on the road, not wanting to see it.

No penis had any right to be alluring when it was flaccid and just flopping. Yet, here she was, after fighting for her life, imagining what it would be like to stroke the limp member to attention.

Raven imagined it would feel like silky steel beneath her palm as she stroked it up and down. Maybe she'd even take the tip of it to her lips…

"Yes," Zane said, not doing anything to cover himself. Shit. Had he heard her dirty thoughts? Was that a shifter gift? "Losing our clothes is something that tends to happen to shifters. They rip and become useless when we shift."

"Cool," Raven mumbled, still trying to clear

her head of all the dirty things she was still picturing. "Think you could cover up?"

"My change of clothes is in the back," Zane answered with a deep frown. "I'm sorry if my nakedness offends you. I don't even get fazed by nudity anymore. I'm too used to it."

That bothered Raven, and she couldn't exactly explain why. Did that mean other women also got to feast their eyes on Zane's perfect, muscular body? Did that mean Zane was used to seeing flawless shifter females, all naked and toned?

Raven rolled her eyes. She might have more curves than the average cover model, but she wasn't going to feel bad about herself because she was sitting next to a human-sized Ken doll. She'd never felt bad about herself, and she wasn't about to start now.

"It's…uh…fine. Not like I don't know what a man's body looks like. I'll just avert my eyes."

For a few minutes, they drove in silence. Raven felt she deserved a medal for sitting there, ignoring Zane and his manliness. It wasn't easy. Her eyes had taken on a mind of their own and they kept wanting to dart back. Even if she had to keep an eye on the road.

How many abs did he have? Was that all muscles in those thighs? And just how thick could a cock get?

No.

She pulled her eyes back to the road and spotted a gas station. She parked the truck in the back away from the street. Or rather, so Zane could put on some clothes in privacy. No one else needed to see that work of art.

Zane grabbed his change of clothes from the back of the truck and slid on a pair of jeans and a green tee. Raven didn't want to mourn the lost sight of his abs, but Zane made the shirt strain in the most delicious way, so at least there was that.

"Hop back in the truck," Zane ordered. "We can't just stay out here in the open like this."

Raven wanted to argue with him and take offense to the fact that he had given her a command. But she couldn't. Not after the showdown in the street in front of the store.

"Holy…shit. Zane. They were going to kill me. Like, full-on attack me in the street. In broad daylight."

She slumped in the passenger seat as the realization crashed into her.

"Yes, I am sorry for that," Zane said, putting a

hand on her thigh after taking his seat behind the wheel. "I was wondering when the shock and panic would take adrenaline's place. Are you okay?"

"I think so?" It sounded more like a question because it was.

Raven didn't know if she was okay.

She replayed the last thirty minutes of her life, completely stunned by the events she had just survived. Zane drove away from the gas station, and Raven didn't pay any attention to where they were going until the scenery out of her window changed.

They were driving out of Salem.

"Hey, just where are we going?" she asked, panic tingling in the pit of her stomach.

"Some place safe. The order won't think to look for you there. I promise you will be safe."

"Where? And what about Cerise? Astra and Selene are still out there, too. They're witches, they'll be targets, too. We need to go get them."

"Every witch from the Bishop bloodline is under protection. Don't worry."

"Don't worry? I was shot at, and my twin sister and cousins are out there. Sitting witches. You need to turn back to get them."

"Raven," he said, squeezing her leg. "You need to listen to me. All three of them are with a member of my team. Wolves, like me. They'll be safe. You'll all be kept in separate safe locations."

"Why are we separated? Wouldn't it make more sense to keep us together?"

Zane gave her a side-eye. "Do you think it's a good idea to keep all of you Bishops in one place like sitting ducks like you said? All we know is that the four of you are the first intended targets. Keeping you apart and away from Salem is the best plan we could come up with on such short notice."

Raven took her phone out of her back pocket and unlocked the screen. She was surprised it was still there and intact after all that she'd been through. Her favorite black skinny jeans had a hole in the knee now. She picked at the threads with her fingers as she scrolled down her contacts to get to her sister's number.

"Gimme your phone," he ordered.

Thinking he needed it to make a better plan on how to deal with the psychotic order, Raven slid her device into his hand and watched as he chucked it out of the window.

"What the heck!" she screamed, turning in

her seat just in time to see the smartphone smash on the road. "What did you do that for?"

"We have no way of knowing if they're tracking you with your phone. Do you have any idea how easy it is to get someone's location from those stupid smartphones?"

As he spoke, Zane reached inside the glove compartment and took out an old flip phone. The small compact silver thing was so small, Zane could have crushed it in his palm if he wanted to.

"This is the only phone we can use."

She took a deep breath and let it out slowly. "Well, that's all fine and good, but I don't know her number by heart."

Frustration rolled off her in tidal waves. Zane might be a hot wolf who had saved her life, but he had just destroyed the only line of communication she had with her sister and her cousins.

And this guy was her mate?

No way. *Yes way*. Stupid hormones. No. Fuck no. She would never give her heart to him. Not after that. Raven crossed her arms and imagined locking her heart far away where Zane would never find it. Let's see how long that lasted.

CHAPTER NINE

ZANE

Zane gripped the steering wheel that much tighter.

"I can't believe you threw my phone away. I didn't even get a chance to call someone to lock up my shop."

"I'll have a deputy handle it."

She pressed her lips into a tight line. "Thanks."

He couldn't quite believe what he had just done. He'd thrown Raven's phone straight out the window without warning her or thinking the action through. He could tell she was annoyed with him. Her arms were crossed over her chest, and she was tapping her foot rapidly.

Every ten seconds or so, her head would whip

to stare at him. She would sigh heavily and turn her head forward again.

"You know what?" she said, sitting up straighter in her seat. "No. This is crazy. I won't have this. Turn this car around right now and take me to my house. I need to see my sister." She gave him a pleading look full of worry and he knew she truly wanted to ensure her family was okay. But he was going to have to let her down.

"I'm sorry, Raven, but no, I can't do that."

She blinked. The worry in her eyes turned to shock and then back to frustration. "I swear," she said through clenched teeth, "if you don't take me to my house right now, I will jump out of the car."

Zane's head snapped to Raven, his eyes wide. Her hands were already clutching the handle with a determined look in her eyes.

He sensed her fear climbing along with her determination. His wolf demanded he slam on the brakes, lest she actually decided to leap out of a moving vehicle.

"Don't be silly. You'd kill yourself. If you just calm down…"

Raven gasped and then glared at him. Zane had the vague memory of a few females in the pack mentioning there was nothing worse than being told to calm down.

"Sorry," he backpedaled. "I didn't mean to say that you shouldn't be upset. Obviously, you have every right to be upset. I just meant that hurting yourself is not the answer. Going to your apartment isn't the answer. Your sister won't be there. She's already in protective custody with someone I trust with my life. It's too dangerous. The Order has already attacked your place of business. The other logical place to look for you is your home."

"Fine. I get it. But you can take me to my condo." She grumbled under her breath. "Please."

Zane took a deep inhale to ground himself. "Raven-"

"You'll be with me. I'll be safe," she said. "I understand you're trying to protect me, but I'm not used to that."

The air in the cab of truck was tinged with fear. She was truly scared for her family and he understood that. He knew she didn't know him and was being forced to trust him without being sure of his intentions.

There was no way Raven would actually

jump out of the car. He could tell, but he wasn't taking that chance. His mate disliked him already. All because of how he had handled the situation.

And he also didn't want to cause her any more distress than she was already feeling. With a resigned sigh, Zane pulled the truck onto the curb and turned to face her.

"If we go to your condo, you have to listen to me. If I spot any danger, you have to follow what I say. I have wolf instincts, so I might sense danger before you."

"Fine," she said, but there was deceit there.

"You know shifters can smell a lie, right?"

"Oh." Raven's face fell. The frustration in her features was replaced with concern. "I'm worried about my family. So I will make an effort to defer to you. But I don't have to like it."

"That's fair."

Zane turned the truck back around, drove through Salem, and straight to Raven's place. He was barely parked when the woman vaulted out of the car, going directly against what he had told her.

"Fuck," he hissed, chasing after her. "Would you just let me go ahead of you in case there's danger?" he called out, trying to sense if they were being watched.

"I know my way. So, no," Raven shouted over her shoulder.

Figures his mate would be a stubborn, independent woman who wouldn't appreciate his chivalrous, protective instincts. Raven bent down, grabbing a hidden key from under a fake rock. He shook his head. He'd have to talk to her about the dangers of hide-a-keys later.

But when Raven put the key in the lock, the door pushed open. It was then that Zane noticed the lock and been broken.

"Raven," he growled, "step behind me." He was sure that whoever had broken into the house was no longer there, but that didn't matter. He wanted to be the first in. Just in case. He wasn't taking any chances with his mate.

"But—"

"Raven." Her name was a warning that time, and with a resigned sigh, she ducked behind him.

Zane pressed on, and he groaned at the sight.

"Oh, no!" Raven's shoulders slumped as she rushed past him.

Every surface was covered in debris. Whoever had been through the condo had wanted to cause as much destruction as possible. One of the windows was shattered. Frames had been ripped off the walls, the pictures laying torn on the ground. There were slashes in the wall, made by some kind of hunting blade. The stuffing had even been removed from the large sectional that took up most of the living room.

"Thank god you weren't here when this happened," Zane mused out loud.

"But Cerise could have been…"

Raven rushed to the other rooms of the house, Zane quick on her heels. They didn't find any sign of Cerise, but Zane knew his alpha had been there. He could recognize his friend's scent anywhere.

"She's safe. She's with a very trusted associate of mine. No harm will come to her. Now, we need to go."

"I am not going anywhere until I talk to my sister."

"Raven, listen to me. We have to go."

"The Order has already been here. Right?" She gestured to her trashed home. "So, they won't come looking for me here."

"They might. And I'm not taking that chance."

Zane was about ready to throw Raven over his shoulder and take her to the truck by force, but he knew he was on her shit list for throwing her phone out the window. He wasn't about to do more to widen the rift between them.

"Grab a few things, and let's head out."

Raven turned to look at him, tears lining her hazel eyes. They weren't sad tears. It was pure anger he saw there.

"I want the Order of Salem to go down for this. They attacked my store. They destroyed my home. We need to track them down."

She walked down the hall and slammed a door. The sound of shuffling things could be heard, but it wasn't nearly as loud as the sound of his mate crying.

Zane laid a hand on the door and wished he could walk in, take Raven in his arms and make this all better. But the closed door was a clear sign.

She didn't want him.

CHAPTER TEN

ZANE

Zane couldn't just stand there, in his mate's vandalized home, listening to her crying while she gathered a few things.

He had to do something.

He cleaned up the broken window, throwing the shards in the trash. He was lucky enough to find a few empty cardboard boxes with the store's logo on them. He cut them up and patched the hole in the glass as best he could. It would keep any critters out until Raven could get a repairman to replace the pane that had been shattered.

Once that was done, Zane began to pick up a few things, making piles of what was salvageable and what was not. He kept an ear on Raven to make sure she was all right.

When she opened her bedroom door, emerging with a bright pink duffel bag, Zane went to her and insisted on taking the bag from her.

"I'll take it to the truck," he explained, throwing it over his shoulder.

The sparkling unicorn didn't bother him half as much as the look of determination on Raven's face.

"I am not getting back in that truck until I speak to my sister."

Zane took his silver flip phone out of his pocket. He dialed Axel's number but didn't press the final button to connect the call. He knew his alpha's number by heart because Zane didn't rely on the device. He had a hard time understanding why some people were so attached to their phones. He had forgotten that little tidbit when he had chucked Raven's phone out of the window.

He could make it up right then and make the call. He knew it went against the plan he had set up with Axel, but he had to do some damage control. He pressed down on the Call button and put the phone to his ear. His alpha picked up on the first ring.

"Axel, I have Raven, and she is insisting on speaking with her twin."

His alpha sighed heavily on the other line. He gave Zane a brief overview of his own ordeal to get Cerise to safety. Zane's eyes darted to Raven as he listened. At least her twin was safe now. That had to count for something.

"They can talk for a little while," Zane said, "but we need to keep them apart until we take care of this threat. There is no way I'm putting all of the Bishop women in the same place to be picked off one by one," Zane said.

"I completely agree," his alpha said.

In matters of the pack, Zane was the security officer. He deferred to Axel. But when it involved the people of Salem, folks who weren't shifters, it was Zane who had the final say. It was a delicate balance, but one they navigated fairly well. They'd done it for years.

This particular situation was odd, however.

It was a mix of supernatural and human affairs. And now the whole mate thing was thrown in, just to really fuck with them.

"I'll take Raven to that place, you know the one, then I'll check it with you. Maybe by that time, the others will have a better handle on these lunatics. We need to know everything about them.

I still have my people at the station looking into them."

"And I have some of the other wolves doing recon, as well. Blaze also has a few of his people on it. We should get this settled in a day or two."

"Here's Raven," were Zane's final words to his alpha.

He passed the phone to his mate, who jumped on it, her face flushed with worry and relief.

"Cerise?" Raven asked.

"Holy mother fucking shit." Cerise's voice was so loud that Zane could clearly make out her side of the conversation. "Raven, they trashed the house. Are you okay? Is the store all right?"

"I saw the house. The store was fine when I left it, but we were attacked there, so we had to leave before I could check for any damage. There might be a few bullets lodged in the brick and mortar. How about you? Are you okay, Cerise?"

"Meh. I'm fine. Axel is just about the grumpiest dude I have ever had the displeasure of meeting, but whatever."

"Focus. We need to figure this out. I have no idea what is going on. Let's compare notes. What do you know?"

"Do you think we should do a spell to—"

Cerise was cut off, and Raven eyed Zane suspiciously.

"This is Axel. I'm the one taking care of your sister for the moment. It's best if you ladies don't perform any sort of magic. Not until this is all over. Is that clear?"

"Listen, buddy," Raven growled, "I don't know who you think you are, but telling witches not to use their magic to protect themselves is a pretty dumb thing to do. We use our magic for good. And to make sure we survive whatever attacks come our way. Now, put my sister back on the phone."

Zane couldn't believe how Raven was speaking to the alpha. Clearly, she had never seen the man. He could be quite intimidating. Zane himself had never been on the receiving end of one of his alpha's nasty stare-downs, but they were the stuff of legend.

"Raven, it's for the best. What if the Order can track your magic?" Axel said to her.

"That's ridiculous," Raven said, rolling her eyes.

"Maybe not," came Cerise's voice over the phone's speaker. The sound of loud shuffling come through the air. A smack and a thud were heard. "I was doing magic at the house. I think that's how they tracked me down."

"But that would mean that they also have some kind of magic," Raven argued. "It's probably a huge, weird coincidence. Cerise, tell whoever this Axel dude is to take you where I'm going." She looked at Zane expectantly, but he shook his head.

"It's best if we all keep to our own hiding spots for now," Zane said. "I'll call you later, Axel."

Before Raven could say anything more, he took the phone from her hand and ended the call.

"I really do not like you," she said to him, venom in her tone. "You might think I'm your mate, but I will never be with a man who keeps me from my sister. I will never fall in love with someone who stops me from using my magic again. If you didn't have that fancy sheriff badge, I would put a spell on you so fast, you wouldn't even know what hit you. But assaulting an officer is a federal offense, so I'm choosing to back down," she grit her teeth. "But I still hate you."

Zane felt a pang in his heart. Her words stung, especially since she didn't understand what it was like for him to feel every particle in his body calling to her. Raven had no idea that the moment he laid eyes on her in her store, he had been done for. Every little action he took, even the ones that set her on edge and angered her, they were purposefully to protect her.

If Raven hated him for it, then he would have to be resolved to that. Let her hate him then, but at least she'd be alive to do it. He would tuck away whatever little hope he had that her hatred would thaw with time and that she would come to see he was actually a decent man.

At least he could hope.

CHAPTER ELEVEN

RAVEN

Raven stood in her trashed condo, her heart heavy and her head aching. Her day had started off so normally. She'd had breakfast with Cerise and then headed to work for the morning shift. Had she known her day would go from good to bad to the absolute worst, she would have stayed in bed.

Not that it would have helped any.

The Order of Salem would have found her regardless.

None of this was Sheriff Zane Cross's fault, and yet here she was. Ripping into him.

She hated him?

Had she actually said those words to him? Yup. Judging by the frown on his handsome face, she had definitely said those words out loud. It was too bad she had because she didn't mean it. Not really. God, not even a little.

What she hated was that there was actually a psycho order of witch hunters after her and her family. What she was distraught over was that her life had been upended.

Sure, Zane had thrown her phone out the window. And yes, he was keeping her from her twin. But he was just reacting poorly to a very weird situation. Not that Raven was going to take the words back. They hung between them like a huge awkward reminder they were nothing but strangers. She felt like a hormonal teenagers. She had to get her shit together.

She shook her head, trying to clear her thoughts, but her eyes caught the cardboard box patched over the broken window. Her heart sped up and slowed in the same second.

"You fixed the window?" Raved asked, completely incredulous.

She was particularly nasty to the sexy wolf sheriff. She really was acting like a little kid with a crush.

She couldn't help it. Ever since he had walked into her store, her entire life had been turned around. Even her phone had suffered. Though after seeing his old as fuck flip phone, it made a bit more sense. He clearly didn't buy into the whole technology thing.

Still. That didn't mean she would forgive that messed up slight.

But he had fixed the window.

After she had railed at him, after she had slammed the door like a teenager in the throes of a temper tantrum. Before she said she hated him. Maybe he regretted fixing the window after that particular comment. Raven needed to keep her witch temper under control if Zane was going around doing sweet things for her even when she was irate. He really made her hormones go all out of whack.

"I can't believe you did that," she whispered to herself as she walked toward the patched-up window.

That was one less thing to worry about just then. The cardboard would hold for a day or so while she got someone in to replace the damned thing.

"It was nothing," Zane said with a shrug. "Least I could do." He gestured to the rest of the space. "Once this is all over, I'll get you to fill in a police report so you can claim the damages on your renter's insurance."

"Huh. The sheriff was with me when I came upon the scene of the crime. That has to count for something, doesn't it?" Her laughter was dry. "If my claim is signed and sealed by the sheriff, they'll have to approve it. No millions of email and phone calls." At least, that's what she was hoping.

"Raven, I know you don't like me, but I need you to trust me when I say I have your best interest at heart. If you don't believe me as a wolf, as a man, at least think of the badge I wear to work every morning."

Raven swallowed loudly.

The man had a point. He had been elected sheriff because the people of Salem loved him. Raven hadn't voted, nor had she paid any attention to the election, but it still spoke for something that the townspeople trusted him with the safety of their town. Could she trust him to keep her safe?

She didn't really have a choice. She could stay alone here in the trashed house, or she could go with him and be safe. With him, at least, she had a direct line to Cerise.

There was the added bonus that if any of the Order of Salem members dropped by, she had a wolf with her.

"Fine," she said with a deep sigh. "Take me to your leader."

Zane looked at her, puzzled by her words.

"Shit, it was a bad joke anyway. Take me to safety. I put my life in your very annoying and bossy hands." She couldn't help but add that. It was easier being mean to him than to think about the way he made her heart flutter.

If she kept her distance emotionally, then it wouldn't matter that Zane claimed she was his mate. He wouldn't want a surly witch with a bad attitude.

"Thank you."

Zane's response took her completely by surprise. She'd expected a victory lap, but not this sweet look that made his green eyes all tender and soft. It made her skin feel hot that he was looking at her like that.

Like she was a prize that he simply had to protect.

Raven hadn't been looked at like that. Her ex-boyfriend Arthur, a man she'd been with for over six years, had never been so caring. She licked her lips, which were suddenly dry, and she looked away.

"I'm sorry for being difficult to deal with." No, stop talking. "I'm just not used to being targeted by witch hunters." Don't explain yourself. "I don't mean to be so bitchy." Yes, you do. Better be bitchy than all gooey for him.

"I understand. This day has been a bit crazy." Zane gave her shrug and walked to the door.

He opened it for her, her pink bag still on his shoulder, and he motioned for her to follow him.

For a few seconds, Raven looked around the condo. This place had been her home but for a few shorts months. She'd moved in with Cerise after the Arthur thing had crashed into a big pile of shit. But it was still home.

If she walked out the door, she was acknowledging the attack at the store this morning had actually happened. It was a lot.

"Where are we going?" she asked, with a resigned sigh.

"Someplace safe, I promise."

Raven walked by him and watched as he locked the door and pocketed the spare key.

"Do you think I'm going to let you keep my house key?" she asked, walking toward his truck.

"It's better than having it in a hollow rock," he grumbled, getting into his vehicle. "Do you know any many calls I go to where the robber gets in with a hidden key? Too many for comfort."

"I didn't realize Salem was such a dangerous place to live," she shot back.

Zane's head snapped to her, eyebrows raised.

"You know, apart from orders looking to kill witches, I mean."

"Yeah," Zane mumbled. "Not like that's dangerous at all."

For a few moments, they were quiet. Raven lay back against the headrest and took deep breaths. She reached inside of herself, trying to find her magic, but it still seemed to be in short supply. If she still had her phone, she would have done a bit of research on how to magnify her power. Or at least to find out how to replenish it faster.

She'd never run out of magic before. She'd also never been under attack before. This was all so new. Raven knew she had to somehow grow her power.

"You okay?" Zane asked. "You're quiet, and that kind of worries me."

"Huh?" Raven was genuinely confused by his question.

"Well," he said, "I've only known you a few hours, but I get the impression that you're not usually quiet. So I'm just checking."

He looked at her briefly, still needing to keep an eye on the road.

Raven was completely taken by surprise by his words. His concern was a stark contrast to how Arthur used to treat her. In their six years together, had her ex ever been concerned when she went quiet? No. In fact, Arthur loved it when she went silent. He said it gave him peace from her constant chatter.

The realization made her skin itch.

"I'm fine," she assured him.

But she wasn't so sure about that. She didn't want to think about how it felt to have Zane worried about her. Not him, the sexy sheriff, wolf shifter who had called her his mate.

Her heart was on lockdown, and there was no way she was letting him in.

Not even a little bit.

CHAPTER TWELVE

RAVEN

"You still haven't told me where you're taking me," Raven said for the millionth time as the scenery of fields and bush passed them by in the speeding truck. It all looked very familiar, but she couldn't tell why. She never really left Salem, never left her town at all, actually.

She took a long, loud slurp from the smoothie she held in her hands, making sure to be as annoying as possible. It didn't even seem to faze Zane's wolf hearing that she was being purposefully noisy.

Raven didn't like playing at being as annoying as possible. Half because she thought it would get

Zane to tell her where they were going. Half because she was aggravated.

And who could blame her?

Her house was trashed, she didn't know how her business was doing, and she was separated from her twin and cousins. She was in a hot, strange man's car on the way into the mountains.

That was a lot to happen in the span of one very shitty morning.

"We're almost there," Zane promised her for the fifth time since they'd started driving.

He wasn't all grumbling orders and grumpy commands.

When Raven had complained of hunger and expressed the need to use a bathroom, he had pulled over at a service station. While Raven had used the facilities, Zane had gotten her a fruit smoothie.

How the man had managed to guess her favorite flavor—mixed berries with a splash of citrus—she didn't know. Arthur had never bothered remembering these little details about her. He would always get her the wrong flavor of ice cream, the wrong coffee order.

Zane had guessed. It was maddening that he

was so attentive, but also so hardheaded all at once.

"How do I know you're not taking me to the mountains to kill me?" Raven asked a few moments later. "How do I know this isn't all a very weird ruse to get my sister and me?"

"You saw my badge," Zane answered. "Besides, if I was going to kill you, would I really take the time to feed you?"

If he hadn't cracked a smile, Raven would have missed the fact he was being silly.

"Holy shit, Sheriff Serious. Was that a joke?"

Zane shrugged. "I don't know. Was it?"

She narrowed her eyes at him, trying to contain her smile. It was a fail, and her heart gave a little bit of thud. Where was the hardened organ who would reprimand her every time she dared to appreciate anything about Zane?

Right. It was busy melting at the sight of Zane's smile. Raven loved the way his sweet grin was completely at odds with his square jaw. She had the sudden urge to cup his cheek to taste his full lips.

"How's that smoothie treating you?" he asked, cutting the sudden tension filling the cab of the truck.

"It's absolutely delicious. Thanks." She punctuated the thought with a long sip of her drink, hoping the loud sound would shake her out of the spell he seemed to be casting on her.

Zane had put on a pair of faded blue jeans and a green tee that brought out the alpine color of his eyes. Raven didn't know if he looked better in his uniform or in layman's clothes.

Or naked.

She definitely couldn't forget that she had seen him completely naked. That had been a good view, too.

"What's going on in that beautiful head of yours?" Zane asked, his smile still playing on his lips.

"Plotting your demise," she answered.

Zane's laughter filled the cab of the truck.

"Maybe wait until you're safe in my cabin to plot any sort of evildoings."

"Your cabin?" Raven couldn't help but have her curiosity piqued by this. "You're taking me to your own place? Is that really protocol?"

"Fuck protocol," he growled softly. "I am not waiting for all of the red tape to be cleared to take you to safety."

"Huh?" Raven was genuinely confused.

"There are very specific ways to deal with someone who is under attack like you are. There are proper channels that must be followed. Think of how people who are stalked get handled. The laws are better than they were a decade ago, but you'd still need to prove you were in danger to get a cruiser parked outside of your place for protection.

"So it's not like I could use those rules of conduct to protect you. I'm sure that conversation wouldn't have gone over too well with my superiors. I can't tell them I'm a wolf shifter, or that you're a witch. That would expose us and it would be entirely too dangerous. They would have asked for proof that you were in danger. They would need a series of documented escalated events. But there was none of that."

"No, there wasn't," Raven agreed. "You just barged into my life, and everything went to shit."

"A teen came into the station early this morning. He told Axel and me everything about his father's plan. Or at least, everything he was privy to, which wasn't very much. That's how I was able to pull you out before anything bad happened."

"My house was trashed," she pointed out. "I was shot at."

"But you're unharmed. If the kid hadn't come forward, we would have been fucked. I would have lost…" Zane stopped himself.

Raven wanted to ask him to go on, but she could tell she wouldn't want to hear what he had to say. It would be about the mating stuff, and she really wasn't down for that.

Zane clearly believed in all that mate connection thing. And he would. That was a big thing for shifters if her very limited knowledge of them was correct. It didn't mean that she had to buy into any of that, however.

Especially not after what had happened with Arthur.

Raven believed in her magic, and she definitely believed in the powers bigger than her that had made her magical talent possible. So she could understand how Zane could be attached to anything shifter related.

But there was one memory she had in her head, one she couldn't exactly shake.

Raven and Cerise had been tiny little witches, barely coming into their powers, and they'd performed a spell to learn who their true loves were. They wouldn't have been curious had they not been watching princess movie after princess movie. In those flicks, the princess was intent on finding her one true love with love's first kiss.

Curiosity and excitement had spurred them on. They'd done the spell, and they had gotten the initials of their true loves. Cerise had gotten ZC, and Raven had gotten AB.

Arthur Banning had been anything but her true love.

It was the one complaint she'd had about magic and spells. They'd probably done it wrong, in their youthful inexperience, but when Raven had met Arthur, her heart had pounded just a little bit faster because of his initials. And maybe that's why she had stayed with him for a bit too long.

Because she believed Arthur was hers.

Because she thought she could make it work.

Because she ignored her instincts that screamed at her every time he came out late.

So yeah, Raven believed in magic. But she didn't know if she believed in true love, in mates. It seemed like a foolish little girl's dream.

CHAPTER THIRTEEN

ZANE

The last two hours of the drive up to his cabin were pretty quiet. Raven seemed to be deep in thought, and though Zane longed to know what the hell she was thinking about, he didn't want to intrude. His mate had been through one hell of a morning, and he didn't want to add to her stress by crowding her space.

He didn't know how to behave around her.

Zane had had a few girlfriends through the years. It had been temporary relationships, something he always knew when he started dating these women. His wolf hadn't even been stirred by any of them. He'd actually come to doubt he would ever find his true mate.

Of course, it would happen at the most inconvenient of times.

And with a witch.

Zane wondered how that would work when they got together. If they got together.

Raven's words were still weighing heavy on him. She had flat out told him he should absolutely not expect any sort of positive feelings from her. But when she looked at him, his wolf perked up, and he was sure he could smell longing in the air.

He wouldn't push her.

He'd wait for things to calm down, and maybe then Raven would be more receptive to seeing him in a more positive light.

The dirt road up to the cabin was a bumpy mess. It didn't matter how many times he tried to smooth out the road, come every spring, more ruts and rocks would ruin his hard work.

The log cabin had been in his family for a long time. It had been his grandparents' home, then it had become his father's hunting cabin. In the years since becoming a sheriff, it had become Zane's safe place.

He was lucky enough that Axel let him retreat here for a few days every couple of months or so.

Tending to the safety of the entire town and his pack wasn't easy work. He was often vilified as a harsh rule-maker. But up here, in the crisp mountain air, he could be just a man. Just a wolf.

"It's beautiful," Raven whispered when the small home came into view.

Zane couldn't help but to be pleased that she liked it.

He watched as Raven hopped out of the truck. She bent down, folding her body in half before springing back up with her hands stretched out to the sky. The content moans that escaped her made Zane perk up with attention. He felt like a creeper for enjoying the show, but what else was a man to do when his mate was moaning and moving her body in the most delicious ways?

She took a few steps toward the cabin, and Zane tried to see if it from her eyes.

The small rectangular shape had a raised wraparound porch that framed the entire cabin. The dark wood was old, but Zane had always taken good care of his cabin.

Raven walked up the two steps and let her hand run along a rocking chair. That particular spot was one of his favorite places to sit to watch the sunrise in the morning.

"This place is yours?" she asked, her eyes going to his in surprise.

"Yup. And it was my parents' before that. My grandfather built it. It's been in the family a while. I like to come here to unwind."

"When sheriffing gets too hard, this is where you come."

"It is."

"Do you usually bring your kidnapping victims here?

Zane could tell that she was teasing him. Her grin was a crooked little thing that pulled one of her eyebrows up in a perfect arch. But he didn't like the tone, nor did he care for the word kidnapping.

"Don't say it like that," he told Raven, barely keeping the pleading out of his voice. "I am not holding you against your will."

"You kind of are," she shot back with a shrug. "I would prefer if we had stayed in Salem and faced this threat head-on with Cerise, Astra, and Selene."

"That wouldn't have been wise or cautious. I don't know who these people are. They have no criminal records to speak of, and we don't know how many weapons they have and to what lengths they would go to hurt you or your family."

Zane walked by her and unlocked the front door. He rushed in and opened a few windows to let the stale air out and let the fresh mountain air in.

"This just feels like we're running scared," Raven said, following him inside. She dropped her bag by the front door and took a lap around the main room.

The small living room held a couch and two armchairs, all pointed toward the fireplace. The kitchen was a minuscule thing where a square table was framed by three chairs. The fourth had broken a long time ago and never been replaced. They hadn't ever needed it. It was just Zane and his parents.

Then it had been just him.

Raven plopped down in his armchair, the one he always used to watch the fire and tend to the flames. It was odd how she kept being drawn to his favorite spots in the small space.

"So, let me ask you this," Raven said. "Do you know the history of the Salem witches?"

"I know enough to know a lot of people died," he answered.

"My people died," Raven corrected. "And do you know why? Because they believed that their neighbors and their family members would speak up for them. They really thought man was essentially good. They didn't think the town would actually hang them.

"But when the first few witches were hung, the others were too scared to speak up. It was too late." She looked away and into the empty fireplace. "I was thinking as we drove up here, I shouldn't have come with you. I won't make that same mistake my ancestors did. I won't just sit back and watch as my people are attacked. I want to fight."

Zane took the seat across from her, and he crossed his arms against the idea of Raven fighting again.

"But to fight efficiently, you need to know your enemy. We barely know anything about the Order of Salem. Until we do, lying low is our best option. Do you understand?"

Raven took a deep breath, closing her eyes for a few moments.

"Honestly? No. I don't. If that makes me stupid or naive, fine. But I really think I should be out there defending other witches. I own a magic store, for fuck's sake. If I can't help them defend themselves, who the hell can?"

"This isn't on you. Especially not since they seem to be intent on killing you all in the order in which your ancestors were killed."

"And the other families? Are they getting the same kind of protection I am? Or am I just special because you think I'm your mate or some shit?" There was no venom in her voice. Raven was really just asking a question out of interest. It still irked him.

She wasn't wrong. He was breaking a few rules and protocols placed by his superiors in taking Raven out of town.

And while he was on shift, too.

He made a note to call Betty and get her to fill in the paperwork for his sudden leave of absence.

Zane took a few seconds to formulate how he wanted to respond to Raven. It was clear she was uncomfortable with the idea of being his mate.

"That's not fair," was what he settled on. "You don't know the length to which we have gone to make sure all of the witches of Salem are safe." That was the truth. They'd even gotten help from the wolf pack from the next town over. Axel didn't do that lightly.

"But if you must know, yes. You are getting more attention from me because you're important to me. I can't help it. My wolf and I need to know you're safe. It's a basic need for me to keep you out of harm's way."

"This is messed up, Zane. I don't even know you, and you're talking like you're in love with me. That doesn't sit right with this modern witch."

Zane let Raven's words wash over him. She had a point. He already felt what their connection could be if she only let him in. Raven didn't have that benefit of just knowing. He had to tread carefully if he wasn't going to completely fuck this up. More than he already had.

"I see that," he managed to say. "And I'll try to keep the mate stuff to myself."

"Thank you."

"You didn't let me finish. I mean that for now, I'll tuck that deep inside of me, and I'll try to behave like an officer of the law should behave with someone he is protecting. But when all of this is over? I'm going to want a chance."

"I can't argue with you, Zane. I don't think you understand that you don't have a chance. That was burned down as soon as you said come with me if you want to live and didn't let me fight for the witches of Salem."

Zane inhaled deeply.

That's when it hit him.

The scent of deceit.

Raven was lying to him.

He did have a chance.

Well. That changed things.

Slowly, Zane got to his feet and took a few steps toward her. In the armchair, Raven had to crane her neck to look up at him. He leaned down and put a hand on each armrest, framing her into the plush chair. He took a deep breath in. This time, it smelled like desire. He didn't even try to contain his grin.

Bringing his face in line with hers, Zane made sure Raven was looking into his eyes.

"You say that, Raven. But I'm a wolf. I can tell that you want me as much as I want you."

He placed his lips against her forehead. He didn't miss the way her breath hitched, or the sound of her heart beating fast to match his own.

When Zane looked back into her eyes, he saw everything he needed to.

Hope.

He saw hope.

CHAPTER FOURTEEN

ZANE

Zane couldn't believe what he had just done.

He'd completely invaded Raven's space. He had even kissed her forehead. His lips were still tingling from feeling her soft skin against his. She smelled like roses and a warm summer's day. It was an intoxicating scent. It followed him everywhere, even in the wood shack at the back of the property where he kept the firewood.

He sniffed his shirt, and Raven's smell was all over him. It was enough to drive him insane with desire for the woman who claimed she didn't want anything to do with him. Shit. Had he met Raven under better circumstances, maybe he'd already be with her.

Perhaps if they had met in town or in a bar, he'd have been able to kiss her lips until she moaned for more. He'd have taken her back to his place and made her come in every way possible until she was the most sexually satisfied woman to ever live.

The reality was the polar opposite.

He had to take his time now that they had gotten off to the worst possible start imaginable.

With a grunt, Zane realized there wasn't much firewood. There was only enough for about two weeks. Not acceptable.

Good thing he needed to do something physical and exerting to keep his wolf under control. The damn animal was a howling mess, demanding to be near Raven.

Zane whipped off his shirt and threw it aside before grabbing his ax. He set up a large piece of wood and swung a practice shot before loosing the blade down with all of his strength.

The wood split like butter.

It was partly due to his shifter strength, and also because he had some shit to work out in his head. He might have been using a bit more of his power than he needed to.

Zane glanced back to the cabin. Raven was in

there, no doubt fuming that he had kissed her. He'd give her space to think about that soft embrace. Maybe giving her distance to figure out why she said she hated him, but called out to him with her body, was a good idea.

He definitely needed to chill the fuck out before he did something more.

Like kiss her. A real kiss.

Even that was nothing compared to what he wanted.

Zane wouldn't think of Raven's long dark hair. Or the way her hazel eyes seemed to sparkle. Or the way her curves filled out her jeans just so. He longed to see what she was hiding under that loose-fitting top.

Ugh.

That train of thought was anything but helpful and the wood he was chopping wasn't the only wood around. He put all mental images of a naked and willing Raven out of his head.

With every chunk he lopped off into manageable logs, Zane felt calmer. His wolf was still clamoring for Raven, but Zane felt placid. He could totally deal with being in a one-bedroom cabin with his mate for the foreseeable future.

A mate who was intent on keeping her distance.

A woman who was as infuriating as she was enticing.

Zane looked at his work and noticed the sun was setting. Shit. He had been chopping wood for hours. His body was covered in a fine layer of sweat, and he had enough wood to see him to the spring.

He felt bad for leaving Raven alone in the cabin for hours. It wasn't like there was much to do. There was no television, and there might have been a few books and magazines laying around. Hopefully, she hadn't spent the afternoon seething and plotting his death, or worse—an escape.

Grabbing his shirt, he bunched the material in his hands. He rushed toward the cabin and walked in, an apology already on his lips.

The words never made it out of his mouth.

Raven was lying on the loveseat with an old paperback in her hands. It was one of the romance novels his mom had loved so much. Raven put the book down and sat up, her hair mussed and her cheeks rosy.

"Sheriff Lumberjack," she greeted him with that smirk that drove him crazy.

"Sorry," he grumbled, heading into the kitchen where he poured himself a glass of water. "That had to get done."

Raven cocked an eyebrow at him. "Really? You didn't spend the entire afternoon out there to hide from me?"

He shrugged and downed another glass of water to keep from saying anything.

"I'm going to shower," he finally decided, "then I'll cook you dinner."

Zane dug through the freezer and took out a few things to thaw while he was showering. He should have done that the second he'd walked through the door, but he had been distracted by Raven.

There was an easy way to get her out of his head.

Under the warm spray of the shower, Zane closed his hand around his aching cock. He placed his forehead against the wall and shut his eyes, letting the memory of Raven's smell and the way she moved fill his every sense.

He pumped his hand up and down his dick, feeling his climax building at the base of his spine. His release was gaining momentum fast as he pictured Raven's lips, her pretty hazel eyes, and the way she smirked. His balls tightened and he grunted, trying to keep the sound as discreet as possible.

Raven didn't need to know he'd been jerking off to her while she sat in the other room.

Zane quickly toweled himself off and slid on a pair of gray sweatpants and a white tee for comfort's sake. He was planning on cooking dinner and then chilling by the fire. He'd completely forgot to call and check in with Axel, but his alpha had also been radio silent. If Cerise was anything like Raven, the other wolf had his hands full, too, and it was no surprise they hadn't yet had a chance to communicate with each other.

Back in the cabin's main room, Raven had changed into a tiny pair of boxers that barely covered her ass and a loose-fitting sweatshirt. She looked like a sexy present. His wolf urged him to unwrap her.

She was hiding again, and Zane wanted to burn the shirt to see what was under it.

Fuck it all to hell, his cock was already hardening. How that was possible after his shower session, he didn't know.

Or rather, he did. It was because everything about Raven called out to him.

Every single thing about her made him crazy in the best way. In the worse way.

It was going to be a long night.

CHAPTER FIFTEEN

RAVEN

Raven watched as a very relaxed-looking Zane moved around the small kitchen. Those sweatpants should have looked absolutely ridiculous on him. But they were slung low, and when he moved his arms, a strip of smooth, gold skin peeked out. She wondered what it would feel like to run her fingers there. Would she feel the corded muscles hiding under the skin? She'd bet she would.

"Give me something to do," she said, leaning against the counter.

Zane took a deep breath and ran a hand along his jaw. "You're my guest. You shouldn't have to work for your supper."

"But I'm bored."

And she was. Raven had spent most of the afternoon trying to replenish her magic with meditation and every other trick she could think of. But she needed a few supplies to be able to practice her craft.

"There wasn't much to do in here while you were busy playing Bush Man. I only started reading that book because I couldn't do anything else to keep myself from going crazy."

Watching Zane as he chopped wood had been an absolutely terrible idea. She'd seen how the muscles in his forearms and back strained when he brought the ax down. How he moved with speed and agility as he chucked the logs into a pile. His ass had looked like perfectly smooth globes as he leaned down to organize the timber into cords.

It had been pure lumberjack porn.

Raven had to force herself to look away from the window because she was about ready to leap down the steps and into his arms. She hated that it had been so erotic to watch Zane work. She wanted to blame her hormones and the fact that she hadn't had sex in a long time. That would have been a cop-out.

It was simply because Zane was a fine specimen of a man.

Actually, he was hands down the hottest man Raven had ever seen. She'd gotten an eyeful of his nakedness in his truck that morning, and that had been something. But seeing his body at work made her think of all the other ways his body could work.

Work her.

Bring her to climax.

Chill, girl. She had to reprimand herself for those stray thoughts. She wasn't looking for a relationship. And it definitely wasn't like she could just fuck Zane for something to do. He believed she was his mate. Sex would mean something to him that it didn't mean to her.

She might have been mad that he had all but kidnapped her, but she wasn't going to play with his emotions. He seemed to be a good man, and she didn't need the bad karma that would be attached to messing with him.

Zane handed her a bag of frozen vegetables and a pot. "Can you bring these to a boil, please?"

"Sure thing," she said and hastily took the bag from his hands.

She didn't intend for their fingers to touch, but they did.

It sent sparks of awareness everywhere inside her. Just like that dumb kiss on her forehead had. Fuck it all. Did he have to be so potent? Raven rubbed her hand against her leg, hoping to extinguish the tingles that lingered on the tips of her fingers.

It was no use. Not only was her hand in a tizzy because they had barely touched, but her forehead was burning from the memory of his kiss. It wasn't just about the kiss, though. It had been the way he had caged her in her seat, invaded her space. She hadn't felt threatened. Not in the slightest. She'd felt needed and desired like never before. In the moment, she had hoped he would lower his lips to hers to give her a real kiss.

But he hadn't. The wolf had run scared, metaphorical tail tucked between his legs. To be fair to him, she had told him she hated him, that she would never be with him. Why had she said those things?

Oh, right.

Because of Arthur and the way that asshole had completely ruined her heart forever.

Raven took a deep breath and focused on the

task at hand. She dumped the veggies in the boiling water and kept an eye on them. Once they were a vibrant color, she strained them and dug out some garlic butter from the fridge. She mixed a dollop of it in the broccoli, cauliflower, and carrots, hoping that the tang of garlic would mask any freezer burn.

Zane moved around her, getting the rest of their meal ready. She noticed he kept brushing up against her. After the first two incidents, she stopped thinking it was accidental and saw it for what it was. Deliberate gestures.

Her entire body was on fire from the tiniest of grazes. Her skin was heated from his arm brushing against hers. Her chest felt tight from where he had picked off a stray strand of her hair.

It was the most chaste, slowest seduction in the history of the world.

And she was falling for it.

She didn't want to. Her heart couldn't take any more abuse than it already had at the hands of Arthur. But her body had other plans. That part of her was down for all the touches. All the looks. All the innuendos.

When dinner was ready, and they were finally

sitting at the small table, Raven was relieved. She would have a reprieve from all of his attention. Maybe it would give her flesh the chance to cool the fuck down so her head could take some control back.

Zane, however, had other plans. He cut into his steak and was barely done swallowing it when he turned his eyes to her.

"Tell me why you always wear baggy shirts."

The words felt like a shot in the tiny cabin.

"Always?" she shot back. "You've seen me in two outfits. That's hardly always."

Zane shrugged, taking another bite of his dinner. "Considering I've only seen you wearing two shirts and both had been way too big for you, that counts as always to me."

Raven rolled her eyes and tugged at her sweatshirt. The damn thing could probably fit Zane and her at the same time. She could try to lie and say it was a comfort thing, but it was no use. Zane was a shifter, and he had told her he could smell lies.

That particular memory would always be fresh in her mind. He had been all up in her space.

Raven had to go with the truth. Maybe then,

Zane would lay off. He'd see the hurt, he'd see how she was damaged and leave her be.

"My ex was an asshole." She tried to sound as nonchalant as possible. "He always commented on my pudge." She patted her stomach through her shirt for emphasis, as if he could see it with his keen shifter eyesight. "So I started hiding it to avoid fighting with him about it. It was just easier that way. Then I guess it got comfortable to hide."

Zane's eyes darkened, and he leaned toward her. "He what?"

"It was nothing," Raven shrugged.

It had most definitely not been nothing. Arthur had given her a full-blown complex about her stomach. It got so bad that toward the end of their relationship, she had taken to wearing tank tops when they fucked. If they ever fucked. Their sex lives had taken a sharp nosedive. Now Raven knew it was because he was getting it elsewhere, but at the time, she hadn't known that.

"Do not defend a man who made you feel like you were anything less than perfect."

"Stop, it's fine. I know I'm far from being the image of dainty feminine beauty. I mean, I know I'm pretty. And I'm mostly confident and pleased with my looks. But Bishop women, we're made curvy. It's the way it is."

That was the truth.

She hadn't doubted herself or her looks until Arthur. It pissed her off that he still had any sort of pull inside of her mind. Truth be told, she hadn't even realized she was still hiding. Not until Zane pointed it out.

How perceptive could a man be?

He had garnered more truths about her in a day than Arthur had in six years. *Maybe that's a mate thing?*

Raven shivered against whoever that voice in her head was. There was no way she was buying into this shifter mate nonsense. She was a witch. Not a wolf.

"Curvy ass witches," she added, injecting as much humor as she could in her voice. She even tried to crack a smile, but the look on Zane's face told her he wasn't buying her bullshit.

He surprised the hell out of her when he pushed his chair back and came to stand in front of her. For a second, Raven thought he was about to do that cage thing she had so enjoyed that afternoon.

But that's not what he did.

Nope.

Zane grabbed her hand and placed it on his cock.

Oh, lordy.

It was hard.

Solid. Rock. Steel.

CHAPTER SIXTEEN

RAVEN

Raven gasped.

Her hand was very much on Zane's erection.

She didn't move away.

And her thumb definitely did not trace the outline. Zane's hands weren't even holding hers anymore.

She was leaving her hand there. By. Choice.

"I've been hard for hours because of you, Raven. Even if I jerked off to thoughts of you in the shower. So don't do that. Don't sit there and give in to the doubts that say you're not absolutely beautiful."

His words were so sweet, and his voice was made deeper with need. Raven still didn't pull her hand away, and she was only slightly embarrassed that she'd been cupping his erection for a solid minute.

There was definitely no slickness between her legs.

Nope.

She was bone dry and definitely not affected by the fact that she had made Zane hard for her just by…well, just by being her.

"Raven." Her name on his lips was a husky plea.

She didn't know if it was because he wanted her to remove her hand and or move it or do something.

She swallowed and tilted her head to look into his eyes. The green irises were dilated, and Zane looked like he wanted to devour her. Spread her out on the table and eat her for dinner.

"Zane," she whispered. "Sorry."

She looked away and rubbed her hand on her leg. His cock had felt warm and heavy against her palm. Raven didn't want to think about that. Things had gotten too real, too fast. With trembling fingers, she lifted her plate and took it to the kitchen. She began cleaning up and doing the dishes, and she could feel Zane's eyes following her progress through the kitchen as he kept eating.

There was no way she could down a single thing after that charged moment.

"I'm going to go take a quick shower," she mumbled before retreating to the small bathroom.

The pale mint color of the walls was somewhat soothing. Raven focused on them for a few moments as she tried to calm her breathing and her heart. The damn thing was about ready to climb out of her chest to sit in Zane's lap.

She wasn't about to let that happen.

Raven turned the shower on and let the water reach scalding temperature before she ducked her head under the water. She let the water massage her scalp, hoping it would wash away all thoughts of Zane and the way he made her feel.

Zane.

He'd been in there less than an hour before, jerking off to her.

How the hell was she supposed to take that? As a compliment? Raven knew that's how he had meant it, and she was flattered despite herself. But she couldn't help but to wonder if Zane found her attractive merely because the animal in his head said she was his mate.

How did that even work? How could Zane trust that instinct so blindly?

Well, shit.

She had done the same.

Sure, she had been a kid when she had performed the spell that had given her the initials of her one true love, AB. But she had decided to date Arthur because of it as an adult. She had chosen to stay with him because of it, again, as an adult.

There was something to be said about behaving a certain way because of your species and the specific intricacies that came with it.

Raven let the hot spray of water beat down her back, taking in large puffs of steamy air. She knew it was silly of her to worry about Zane and his mating instincts while there was an order of psychos after her and the rest of the witches in Salem.

Fuck, she hadn't seen her sister since the attacks. And here she was pining after a boy.

No.

That was wrong.

She definitely was not pining. And in no way could Zane be called a boy. He was all man.

Logically speaking, Raven knew she was stuck

in the cabin with Zane. She couldn't do magic yet. Her stock was still depleted. But the second she felt strong enough, she would find a way to communicate with Cerise. Or in the very least, she would have to find a way to track down the Order of Salem.

There had to be some kind of spell she could do that would let her gain some information. Like how many members there were, the amounts of weapons they had, if they were actually able to track magic.

Shit.

Maybe her first step should be to put up wards around the cabin so if she did perform magic, there would be no way for the order to trace her. She'd need salt and lots of it. There was no way Zane had the pounds of salt it would take to protect the cabin. She'd have to convince him to take her to town in the morning.

Once Raven was standing under the lukewarm water, she knew she had overstayed her welcome in the shower. It was time to go back out and face Zane after the very erotically charged moment they had exchanged.

She put her pajamas back on and braided her wet hair back and away from her face. Raven hoped that the braid would tame her wild curls so she could look halfway decent in the morning. She was desperate to understand why she was so at odds with herself about Zane. The wavering between wanting him and pushing him away had to stop. She was really starting to annoy herself.

In the living room, Zane sat by the large fireplace, stoking the fire. He turned to look at her and gave her a bright smile.

"Good shower? Sorry if the water pressure is off. The plumbing is old as sin."

"It was fine, thanks."

She sat on the loveseat, curling her feet under her. Raven had a hard time looking at him. It was difficult to sit there, making small talk about water pressure when she knew what his cock looked like, what it felt like in her hand.

"We should get some rest. You had a crazy day. I bet you're just beat. I'll show you to the bedroom."

Zane stood and held out his hand to her, but Raven shook her head.

"There is no way you're taking the couch. Put the chivalry away, big guy. We both know you wouldn't be comfortable on this particular piece of furniture." She pointed down the sofa. It was bigger than the average loveseat, but there was no way his six-foot-something frame would fold on it.

"Then share the bed with me," Zane purred, leaning toward her just a tiny bit.

Raven shook her head. "Nope. Not going to happen, Sheriff Cocky. I am taking the couch."

She deserved a fucking medal for refusing to share a bed with him. But there was no way she could sleep beside Zane and stay focused on her goal of getting her magic back to fighting levels. Raven had a mission: get her sister and save the witches of Salem. That did not include falling into bed with her protective companion, no matter how hot and endowed he was.

"Sheriff Cocky?" he chuckled, leaning a fraction lower.

Raven swallowed, her eyes glued to his lips. They were right there.

"Raven," Zane's voice had that whole husky thing happening again.

"Yes?" she responded, trying to stay very still as he knelt in front of her.

"I'm going to kiss you."

Zane didn't even give her a chance to protest. He placed his lips on hers, his hands going to her hips.

It was over way too soon.

"That wasn't protection behavior," Raven whispered against his lips.

"It wasn't," Zane agreed, his hands still on her hips.

Raven wanted to push him away. She didn't want to revel in the way it felt to be in his big strong arms. She wanted to hold on to the fact that she was furious with him. She needed to keep being wary of him.

But the attraction she felt was more powerful than her indignation. Raven didn't know if it was actually because she was Zane's mate, but she was having a very hard time keeping away.

She wasn't too sure how, but she was suddenly on the floor with him, and he scooped her up against him.

She didn't pull away when she saw his head lean down again. His trajectory was clear. He was going to kiss her again. And she was going to let him. Again.

The brush of his lips against hers was soft and gentle at first, but when Zane felt her give in to the moment, his movements took on steam. His lips moved against hers, melting away all of her defenses. When his tongue ran along the seam of her mouth, Raven moaned and gave him entry. Their tongues rubbed against each other.

Raven didn't know how or when Zane had lifted her into his arms, when his hands had taken hold of her ass, but she didn't care. She held onto him, her fingers digging into the soft flesh at the back of his neck.

"Raven," he groaned when she moved against him. "I'm sorry. You set a boundary, and I didn't respect it."

"Shut up," she whispered, cupping his face in one small palm. She guided his mouth back to hers.

Raven knew it was ill-advised. She knew that in a few minutes, she would regret this kiss and this momentary lapse in judgment, but at least she would always have the memory of these perfect kisses.

"Okay," he said, putting her down. "I think that we've put each other in enough trouble. Sleep tight, beautiful." He dropped a kiss on top of her head and retreated to his bedroom.

Zane didn't close the door, but he went to the bedroom to change into pajama bottoms. Raven tried to keep her eyes off of him as he walked back to his room, but the plaid material sat so low on his hips, she could track the deep V of his abdomen.

"Night, Raven," he called out from the dark.

"Goodnight," she replied.

In the middle of the night, Raven was still listening to the sound of the cabin settling. Zane's loud breathing streaming in from the next room would have been a comfort if she hadn't been so torn up about the kiss they had shared.

Well, more like kisses.

Raven didn't know what to do with herself.

Zane knew how to kiss, he knew how to touch her. She wanted more. It made her feel silly for making such a big deal about his whole mate deal before. She tossed and turned, trying to find a way to reconcile what she thought about love and how she was feeling for Zane.

Somewhere in there, she had to toss in the actual shitty situation she found herself in. Flipping onto her back, Raven sighed deeply and hoped Cerise was having a better go of it than she was with her protector.

CHAPTER SEVENTEEN

ZANE

Zane turned in the bed, half hoping Raven would have crawled in beside him during the night. She hadn't. He ran a hand across his face, trying to shake the sleep from his eyes. It hadn't exactly been a restful night. He'd been awakened by every single sound, wary of the Order of Salem, and the fear that they would take his mate away before he ever really got a chance with her.

The sounds that kept him up were never an attack, though. Raven moving around on the loveseat made squeaking noises. There was no doubt in his mind she had been uncomfortable sleeping there. He'd have to double his efforts and get her to share the bed with him tonight. If he ended up holding her against him in his sleep, well, then so be it.

Zane couldn't quite believe that they'd shared such a passionate kiss, and Raven had still refused to share a bed with him. While their lips were locked, he had thought he'd made progress, melting his mate's defenses.

He didn't know much about her, but that didn't matter. She was his. And she had been deeply hurt by her asshole ex. Raven had closed her heart off because of the shit this asshole had put her through. If Zane ever met that guy, he'd be in serious trouble.

Now, he had his work cut out for him. He would have to pull out all of the stops to get Raven to see how good they could be together. If he had been more of a romantic, if he had more experience with steady relationships, Zane wouldn't have been so nervous about trying to seduce Raven.

All he knew to do was physical stuff, like be in her space, touch her softly, kiss her. He knew that wasn't enough. Not for his mate, and not for himself. He wanted to know everything about Raven. Even the parts that hurt her to share.

He wanted to erase all her pain, all her bad

times, and replace them with nothing but the best of memories. She deserved that and so much more.

In the living room, Raven was stirring again. Not just because she was restless on the sofa, but because she was fully awake as the sun's light was streaming into the cabin.

Her bare feet slapped against the cold floor, and he watched as she made her way into the bathroom. The shower kicked on, and he sighed.

If they were together, he would be joining her. He'd be buried deep inside her while her legs were wrapped around his middle. He'd suckle her nipples until she cried out his name in pure ecstasy.

Great.

Now his morning wood was that much harder. With a growl, he rolled out of bed and rearranged his cock. It was painful, begging for release. If only he could take care of it with Raven.

The bathroom door swung open as he was prepping the coffee machine.

"Good morning," he said, his voice still raspy from his fitful sleep.

"Hi," Raven responded. "I know it's early, and you've just woken up, but I think we should go get some supplies. We drove by that small town on the way up here. I need a few things."

Zane frowned. He didn't like thinking that Raven didn't have everything she needed. He knew she wanted to be with her twin, but there was nothing for that. He was also aware they would run low on food. The cabin had but the barest of minimums. He kept the small freezer filled, but he was usually here alone, and he usually came to the cabin loaded with groceries.

"What do you need?" he asked, intent on making a mental list. He was debating leaving Raven there while he ran out to do the errands. He couldn't see that going over too well, however.

Raven looked away, avoiding his eyes. "Just some stuff."

A cold realization made its way up his spine. She was plotting something.

"You want to get some stuff to do magic, don't you?" He knew the answer. She didn't even have to respond.

"I was thinking I could put up a few wards around the cabin." She shrugged like it wasn't a big deal. Like he hadn't already told her that she couldn't do magic while they were in hiding.

Zane crossed his arms. He could tell she

wasn't being completely honest. She was keeping something from him.

"Remember, you can't do magic." He needed to say it out loud to reassure himself Raven hadn't forgotten. He was terrified that she'd do magic and the Order would find them. That he wouldn't be able to protect her, his mate. "We still don't know if they can track it."

"But there's no way," she grunted in frustration, her hands going into her hair. "That would mean they have magic, too. Why would other magic wielders want to destroy us? It doesn't make sense."

"Look, let me just shower real quick. I need to think clearer, and it's difficult."

Raven's hair was a long ,wavy mass of dark that made his entire body ache. He wanted to run his fingers through it, he wanted to bury his face in it and memorize the scent. Fuck, he wanted to feel the hair dragging against his chest as Raven rode his cock.

Before he reached out and kissed her senseless, Zane retreated to the bathroom. In the safety of the small room, he took care of himself. Again.

He imagined doing all of these dirty things with Raven. Again.

When he came, hard and fast, he was sure she'd heard his grunt of satisfaction. A twisted part of him was happy for that. Then maybe she would know just how insanely appealing she was to him. She'd understand just how much he wanted her.

Exiting the bathroom, he retrieved his small silver phone from its hiding spot.

He wasn't purposefully trying to keep Raven cut off from the world, but he knew if she had found the phone, she would have called her sister. They would've planned something that would have put them in danger.

He didn't know much about Raven, but he knew she didn't like hiding out while there was a threat out there in the world.

"I have to call Axel," he said, knowing they needed to check in with the pack and his deputies to get the information that had been amassed on the Order of Salem. Maybe if Raven knew more about them, she'd be less inclined to face them.

"Great," she hopped up and rushed toward him.

He made the call, and there was barely a single ring before it was picked up.

"Hello?" a feminine voice asked.

"Who is this?" Zane was confused. He'd really been expecting Axel's voice.

"Cerise," the voice answered.

Right. The twin. Zane wondered how she had gotten the phone away from his alpha. Distracted by the possibilities and how his leader was faring with his own Bishop witch, he didn't see Raven pouncing on him for the phone.

"Cerise?" Raven grabbed the phone out of his hands. "Are you okay?" she asked, "Where are you?" Zane took the device back and placed the call on speaker. It was safer that way. Even though he had shifter hearing, he wanted to make sure he caught any word from Axel.

The light sound of shuffling was heard, and Raven shot Zane a nervous look.

"I'm fine, Raven," Cerise clicked her tongue. "Just like I know you're fine, too."

"Look, I think I know what we need to do to stop this Order of Salem nonsense. I had an idea this morning. If we both do the spell that—"

The line went dead. Zane could guess why that was. The second Raven had mentioned magic, Axel had ended the call. The alpha didn't want any of the Bishop witches to be doing magic at the moment. It made sense.

But that didn't make it any easier for Zane. He had just told Raven that very thing, and she had been none too pleased. Now, compounded to that, she hadn't been able to talk to her sister.

And here he had been hoping that the kisses from the night before had bonded Raven to him.

No chance.

Not with the way she was throwing daggers at him with his eyes. The kisses had been amazing, and truthfully, Zane was having a hard time not mauling Raven right then and there. A man needed some kind of release after having his lips on someone so decadent as her.

"I need to call back," Raven said, diving for the phone. Zane didn't even try to stop her.

She hit the redial button. Zane watched her face morph into a mask of annoyance as the phone rang and rang, and no one picked up.

"I know she was just by the phone, so why isn't she answering?" she asked him as if it were his fault.

"I'm guessing Axel and your sister are having words about magic. Maybe they'll call back when they've settled that."

"No, that is not for Axel to decide. It's magic. That makes it witch business. And seeing as

Cerise and I are the witches, it should be up to us to make a plan of attack."

"Maybe, but Axel is a wolf alpha."

"So? You're the sheriff."

"It's a delicate balance between Axel and me. He takes care of the paranormal, wolf stuff. I am in charge of the human, law things. It works."

Raven crossed her arms. "Does it? Because from where I'm standing, two women are being held by two wolves."

"Four," Zane corrected before he could stop his mouth.

It did nothing to help his situation. Obviously. "My cousins are with wolves, too, aren't they? Not with some of your officers, but with two wolves."

"Yes," he said because he didn't really want to lie to her.

"So I guess I have my answer. Axel is in charge."

Zane didn't mean to bristle at her words, especially not since he had a feeling she was saying them especially to irk him. He took a deep breath.

"Like I said, he is the alpha of the pack. The supernatural is part of his jurisdiction."

"But the Order of Salem are humans. That means you should be point. No?"

"We're a team, actually. There's a reason why wolves live in packs. We all depend on each other, we rely on each other. It's important to be part of a unit, part of a family."

"I get that, you know. That's why I want to be with my sister and my cousins."

A wave of guilt hit him square in the chest.

He needed his pack to live. He should have understood that it would be the same for her. Zane was grappling, trying to find the words to apologize for keeping all of them in different locations, but he came up short.

"We're going to the store," Raven said, crossing her arms, tapping her foot. "And when we get back, we are so calling Axel again. I want to talk to my sister."

Zane knew he had to play for time. He didn't want to go out in the world without checking in with Betty at the station to see what they had learned.

"Before we go to the store, let's go for a walk. I need to shift."

He was about to go full personal.

Zane was going to show her his wolf.

CHAPTER EIGHTEEN

ZANE

Zane knew Raven had already seen his wolf. The fact that she would see it again shouldn't have felt like such a heavy, loaded thing between them.

These were different circumstances, though.

They weren't fighting for their lives.

This shift was something else entirely. He wanted Raven to see his wolf, he wanted her to interact with it so she could understand what it was like for him to be around her. His mate.

How difficult it was for him not to reach out and hold her hand, to kiss her.

Because, fuck, that's all he wanted. Even when she stood there with him, arguing that they should be doing more. He wanted to cup her beautiful face and kiss her full lips until she forgot all of the dangers that lurked for her beyond the safety of the cabin.

"Gimme a few minutes. I really need to call the station and see how they're fairing."

"How do I know you won't call Axel?"

"You have got to trust me, Raven. I need to call my people. They were doing some digging into the history of the Order of Salem. I need to know what they know before we head out. I need to know that you trust me."

She sighed heavily, pinching the bridge of her nose with her thumb and forefinger.

"Do you trust me?" he asked her.

He knew it wasn't fair to ask that of her. They barely knew each other, but he had to know if he was making any sort of headway with her.

"I don't know, Zane," she answered honestly.

Zane nodded. It wasn't a no.

It wasn't a yes, either.

He dialed the station's number and waited for someone to pick up. He tried to tell himself he wasn't making the call in the cabin to prove to Raven he was actually calling his work, but he knew it was lie.

"Salem Sheriff Station, Deputy Betty Armstrong."

"Betty, it's Zane."

She audibly sighed in relief. "Sheriff, we have some information about Robert Griggs, the leader of the Order of Salem." Zane tucked the phone between his shoulder and his cheek, grabbed a notepad from one of the drawers, and headed out to the porch.

He didn't necessarily want to keep things from Raven, but if anything was shocking or disturbing, he didn't necessarily want her to know either. She'd worry more about the other witches, and it would become even harder to keep her in the cabin's safety. At least, now, she knew he hadn't lied to her about who he was calling.

"Go ahead, what did you learn?"

Betty sighed, and he could see her shaking her head like she usually did when she had to recite a perpetrator's laundry list of crimes.

"He was arrested for disturbing the peace for the first time when he was sixteen for staging a protest. I won't even get into those details, but he is a misogynistic asshole. There's a bunch of other misdemeanor charges. Then there are a few more serious things.

"Assault and battery, assault with a deadly weapon. He's done a couple of short stints in jail, but it looks like he has a very good attorney. And that's the weird thing, I can't tell who is fronting the bill for such an expensive lawyer. All I can say is that Griggs seems to have powerful friends with deep pockets."

"How's his kid?"

"He's okay. He's with his aunt right now, and we have a car on them just in case Daddy Dearest decides to try any funny business. He hasn't been seen since the attack on Gemstones, though. And I know he was injured, but he didn't go to the hospital to get treated. Now we have to talk about the history of the Order of Salem."

"I don't like how you said that," Zane grunted.

"You shouldn't. It's bad. They've been around since the time of the witch trials. Around 1694, to be exact. It was a Griggs in charge then as well. The Order is linked to a series of vandalism acts and a few unsolved murders from 1873 all the way up to 1947. Then they got quiet, and it seems they were all but forgotten.

"Jett found something interesting, though. There's an actual social media page for the Order.

It's full of rants and weird stuff. The IP address has been linked to Griggs. The page has quite a few followers, so we're combing through the comments and likes to see who would be a likelier member of the Order of Salem."

"Right, because liking a rant on social media doesn't necessarily mean that you'd be ready to take up arms and attack a group of women."

"Exactly," Betty agreed. "We have six names in total so far. Four men and two women. There's an ABP out for them as persons of interest for the shooting at Gemstones."

"This is all great work, Betty. Thanks. Have you spoken to Axel?"

His deputy laughed. "Oh, yeah, I have. Our fearless leader is being seriously tested by the witch he's protecting. He called to get some advice. That wasn't something I was expecting from the great Axel Barrick."

Zane thought about his own witch and how she tested him, and he couldn't help but chuckle.

"Yeah, well, I'm sure I should also ask for some advice."

"Oh, not you, too," Betty groaned. "What boneheaded thing did you go do?"

"Nothing," he protested. "I mean, beyond

showing up at her store with bad news, throwing her phone out the window, and keeping her at my cabin far from civilization."

"You know, it's a good thing that we shifters have the mate sense. Otherwise, you males wouldn't stand a chance in hell at figuring your own emotions."

"I don't disagree," Zane grumbled.

"Look, it must be stressful for her. Do something nice. Kind. Thoughtful."

"I tried, but she refused to take the bed."

"Zane Cross!" Betty screamed into the receiver. "Are you telling me you made her sleep on the sofa? After you had thrown her phone out a window?"

Zane didn't want to say anything.

"You're an ass. Make it up to that woman, or I swear to god, I will box your ears. I don't care that you're my boss or the pack security officer. If she's your mate, figure your shit out. Now, I need to run the office for you. Is there anything else you need?"

"Apart from the mate stuff, did Axel give you any information?"

"Only that he absolutely hates magic. I think

he's just more afraid of Cerise than he's letting on."

For the first time since meeting Raven, Zane wondered what her twin might be like. Raven was stubborn as hell but still fairly rational. Maybe Cerise was less levelheaded. He hoped, for his alpha's sake, that wasn't true.

"Axel didn't pick up the phone when I called earlier," Zane explained, not mentioning how the first call had abruptly ended at the mention of magic. "If he gets in touch with you, please tell him to call me. We need to formulate a plan beyond what we can do with our badges."

"Yes, Sheriff. Good luck with everything." He could hear the smile on Betty's voice.

He'd known her most of his life, so she got away with a lot more than she should, both as a pack member and as an employee. He hung up and tossed the phone onto one of the rocking chairs.

"Raven," he called out, "want to see my wolf?"

CHAPTER NINETEEN

RAVEN

Raven paced the length of the cabin's main room, watching as Zane spoke on the phone with the sheriff's station. She couldn't make out what he was saying, but she had a feeling he had purposefully started the call where she could hear who he was talking to to gain her trust.

It had kind of worked.

And she really hated admitting that.

So they shared a few kisses and what? She was ready to forgive the fact that he had all but kidnapped her? That she had no way of contacting the outside world without him?

But there had been kisses.

If she was honest with herself, Raven wanted

more. Maybe under different circumstances she would have joined him in his bed during the night. But there was a threat out there, and instead of facing it head-on like she wanted, she was hiding.

She watched as Zane chucked his phone onto one of the rocking chairs sitting on the porch. It brought back a very vivid memory of him tossing her own phone out the truck window.

"Raven," he called out, "want to see my wolf?"

Did she ever.

When she had seen him the day before, it had been in the middle of a battle. She was looking forward to seeing if the wolf kept any of Zane's traits. She seriously doubted the wolf would have green eyes.

She walked onto the porch and down the two steps.

"You won't maul me if you shift?" she asked, trying to sound teasing. But she was afraid it had sounded more irate than anything. She gave him a warm smile to counterbalance her tone.

Zane smiled at her, and it made her skin feel hot. Did he have to be so goddamn hot?

"You're perfectly safe with me, I promise." He

ended his line with a wink, and Raven's knees all but buckled.

Zane kicked off his shoes and bent to take his socks off. She knew he was about to strip out of his clothes, but she didn't know how to look away. Suddenly, her eyes only wanted one thing.

To watch.

He pulled his shirt over his head. The rippling abs were right there. She could reach out and touch them. Raven crossed her arms to keep herself from doing just that.

When he unbuttoned his pants, she made herself looked away. She recalled that shifters ruined their clothes when they took their animal shapes, so it made sense that he would remove the clothing before taking on his wolf form. It didn't make this moment any less erotically charged.

She wouldn't look.

Nope.

Zane pulled his boxers down, and she couldn't help herself. She looked and got an eyeful.

Well, it was only because she really wanted to see what it was like when Zane became an animal. It had nothing to do with the way his gold skin looked in the sunshine. And definitely not because she wanted to memorize every inch of his body for later.

If Zane commented on her looking at him, she knew what she would say. That she had seen the shift from wolf to man, but not the other way around, and that she was curious as to how that worked.

Zane's entire body morphed, sprouting thick gray fur. It looked painful, and Raven actually had to cover her eyes for a few seconds. She didn't like knowing he could be in pain because of the shift. That didn't seem right. His beautiful face melted into a jowl and muzzle.

The transformation complete, he shook out his body, his tail wagging. Okay, so he looked like the cutest husky she had ever seen.

She took a step forward.

"Can I pet you?" she asked, not really knowing if it was rude to ask.

But Zane padded forward and nodded his head. Raven rubbed behind his ear, scratching the thick fur there. A low rumble made Zane's body tremble, and she backed off with a gasp.

Zane gently nipped at her fingers, making it clear he had been growling out of appreciation.

"You are one weird wolf," she laughed, but

she took to petting the top of his head. "So, what now? You go off in the woods to chase a squirrel or two?"

The wolf sniffed and shook his head, making an odd sort of noise.

"Go. Chase your prey. I'll be sitting right here."

Raven took a seat on the steps. Zane took off at a run straight into the thicket that lined the cabin's property. A howl echoed through the air, making a few birds scatter.

She giggled as she saw Zane pounding back toward her with a few wildflowers sticking out the side of his mouth. He dropped the stems at her feet, and Raven knelt down to pick them up.

"You did not just pick flowers for me while in your wolf shape," she mused out loud, running her fingers along the delicate petals.

Sure, there were still some roots and dirt caked to the bottom of the stems, but the gesture had been so sweet, it made her heartache.

She tried to remember when Arthur had brought her flowers, but she was drawing a blank. Maybe in the very beginning of their relationship, but definitely not in the last few years.

Zane padded over to his pile of clothes and

shifted back into his man form. He quickly threw on his pants and bundled the rest of his clothes in his hands.

"I ran the perimeter of the property, and nothing is amiss. We're still safe here."

"Thanks for these," Raven said, taking a step closer to him.

It was her stupid heart making her walk forward. Her head screamed no, no, no; do not fall for this.

"They were so pretty. They reminded me of you."

Wow. Okay.

How was she supposed to resist lines as sweet as that?

The answer was simple. She couldn't.

CHAPTER TWENTY

RAVEN

They were so pretty, they reminded me of you.

Zane's words were simple, but they had landed on her heart like a balm for all of the shitty things Arthur had gotten her to believe about herself.

Raven couldn't quite believe Zane was being so sweet to her. She felt about ready to explode with giddiness. Getting onto the tips of her toes, Raven dropped a quick peck on Zane's cheek.

As if he had anticipated her move, he put an arm around her waist and kept her close to him when she tried to pull away.

"Hey," she breathed, feeling lightheaded so close to him.

He didn't say anything to her oddly placed

greeting. He just lowered his head and placed a soft, sweet kiss to her lips. Another, but this time, he lingered longer, bringing her hips in line with his.

Flowers completely forgotten, Raven put her arms around his neck and lined up her mouth with his so that the next kiss could be deeper.

And, oh my, was it ever.

Zane didn't waste time on the next one.

His tongue plunged into her mouth, exploring her mouth as his hands left her waist to cup her ass. Raven moaned into their kiss and gave as good as she got. Kissing Zane was like sipping on pure lust. It made her knees weak, and made her heartbeat about a million beats per second. He knew just how much tongue to give, how much pressure to apply.

It was like he was made to kiss her.

He was, her heart cried. Because of the mate thing. Right.

Shit.

And she was getting caught up in it. She pushed away from him, panting.

Even though she had been able to break their lip lock, she wasn't able to keep her hands off him. Her palms lay against his chest, and she could feel the insane beat of his heart.

The erection she had felt pressed against her wasn't the only proof he wanted her. His own heart was in on it, too.

No thought had ever been scarier.

Raven needed distance and fast.

"Explain to me what happened on the call with the station. Can I go back to Salem?"

Her words were much more effective than any cold shower.

Zane took a few steps away from her, and his hands went to his pockets as if he didn't trust himself not to reach out for her again.

I'm right there with you, buddy, she thought to herself.

Zane gave her a bit of information on the order, but it was clear by the frustration in his tone, he wished they had more to go on.

"So then…" Raven knew her next words would create a rift between them. She needed that distance between them to exist. She wasn't ready to get her heart all tangled up with another man. Not after the shitshow that had been over a half decade with Arthur.

Logically, she knew that wasn't fair to Zane to keep him at arm's length because of her past. It didn't help that she couldn't see how to keep away from him. That was twice in as many days as they'd known each other that she'd ended up in his arms, grinding against his dick like her life depended on it.

"Then that should mean we're good to get back to Salem. I can be with Cerise and my cousins. We can make a stand at home, all together."

Zane ran a hand over his face, clearly bothered by the change of pace. The man needed to buckle up. She knew her emotions about him were going to give him whiplash if he wasn't careful.

"No, absolutely not. Nothing has changed, Raven. If we keep all of you divided, it spreads out the Order thin. They can't get organized if you're in a bunch of different unknown locations."

"But if we knew what location they were in, we could attack first. Show them we won't let ourselves be bullied or destroyed. Not this time."

"Raven, there are seven confirmed members. We have four witches in four different locations. That means they would have to be in teams of two, maybe three to attack a wolf and a witch. That doesn't sound like a great plan. Keeping you all apart is the only plan we've got."

"But if we were all together, it would be four witches and four wolves against seven humans. And I'm sure your alpha would make more wolves join in on the fight."

"I'm going to ask you something, Raven. And I don't want you to get mad. I just… I want you to understand something."

"Then ask."

"Have you ever been in a fight where death was a possibility?"

"Apart from the one yesterday? No."

"Well, a lot of us wolves have. We don't take it lightly. More than that, there is no way Axel would let Cerise fight and I sure as—"

"You better not finish that sentence, Zane Cross," she warned. "You don't let me do anything. I choose to do things. You can't stop me."

"As my mate—"

"I am not your mate. Don't we have to fuck for that to happen? I mean, in a specific way?"

Shit. She needed to keep it in her pants, or there was a very real possibility she would indeed end up with Zane balls deep inside of her. There was no telling what she would agree to in that moment. Not if the way he kissed was any sort of indication as to how he did other things.

Zane stalked toward her. In that moment, she saw more of the wolf in his eyes than the man. By rights, it should have scared her. It didn't. She knew Zane wouldn't hurt her. The knowledge spurred on her rebellious streak.

"You may not think you're my mate, Raven," he growled, putting his hands on her hips, "but when you kiss me, I can tell you feel it. You're mine, Raven Bishop. You might be a stubborn witch who refuses to see what is between us. But. You. Are. Mine."

Raven didn't even have time to respond.

His mouth was on hers again.

She moved her hands to push him away, but the damned things only clawed at him, bringing him closer to her. This time, there was nothing sweet or tender about the kiss.

It echoed his words. He was claiming her. Making sure Raven knew just how her body responded to him.

And she wanted him.

Fuck, did she want him.

CHAPTER TWENTY-ONE

ZANE

Zane didn't want to stop kissing her. He didn't want to let Raven go. He wanted to take her into his arms and lead her to the bedroom.

But that was exactly the last thing he should do, and he knew it. Raven was unsure about him. Not only his intentions as a sheriff, as a wolf, but also as a man. Every inch of terrain he got with her pushed him back ten paces for the next few hours. It was an unsteady dance that made his heart ache.

He wanted Raven, but there was no way he was going to just take her body. He wanted her heart, as well. And he wanted her to give those to him willingly. Not in the heat of the moment, because she let her physical attraction drown her.

Using all of his self-control, Zane disentangled their limbs and set her a few steps away from him.

"Why did you stop?" she asked before clamping a hand over her mouth like the words had surprised her.

He hissed out a breath and ran a hand through his hair before rubbing at his face. He didn't want to feel the lingering sensation of their kiss on his lips. He needed a clear head to say what he needed to.

"We can't do this anymore, Raven. Not until you stop toying with me. If you don't admit that you want me, if you can't believe in this connection between us, then I'll let you be."

Her face fell, and he had to look away, or he'd bundle her up in a hug to soothe the hurt off her beautiful features.

His wolf thrashed against his mind, growling ferociously.

You've got no right to say those things to her, the animal insisted. *She's ours. Take her.*

Zane would do no such thing. Unless Raven came to him, unless she initiated contact, he would keep his hands to himself. He wanted her more than anything in this world, but he wouldn't play second fiddle to the bad memories in her head. He wasn't her asshole ex, and in time, she would come to realize that.

Maybe then, when she came to him, it wouldn't be against her better judgment.

It would be because she needed him more than air.

That's how Zane felt about her.

The next few days, stuck in a one-bedroom cabin with her, should prove interesting. He needed a distraction and quick. Zane pulled his shirt back on and tied his boots up while Raven watched him. She hadn't said anything, and he didn't know if that was a good thing or a bad thing.

"Let's head into town. We need a bit more food if we're going to survive here. You'll have to disguise yourself, though. Just in case."

Raven shook her head as if she didn't understand his words. He was sure she was merely confused by the sudden change of conversation.

"Disguise?" she asked, catching up and clearly not pleased with the plan.

"Yup," he said. "I have a baseball cap you can wear."

She crossed her arms and narrowed her eyes at him. "Ah, yes. The magic of the baseball cap pulled low onto my head. No one will ever recognize me." Her tone was dripping with sarcasm.

She wasn't wrong, Zane knew that, but he also knew it was better than nothing. They still had very little information about the Order of Salem, and there was no way to tell just how long of a reach they had. He'd take her into town, but he would make sure she was as safe as possible while they were out and about.

In the truck on the way to the market, Raven held the hat on her knees. She'd refused to put it on so far, and Zane had a feeling it was going to be a battle to get her to wear the damn thing.

"You going to put that on or what?" he asked as they drove into the town limits.

"I really don't see why this is necessary. It's not like the Order of Salem will be trolling all of the state's grocery stores on the off chance they run into a witch. We're four hours from Salem."

"Exactly," Zane argued. "We are only four hours away from Salem. That means we could be surrounded by the ancestors of the people who lived in Salem. Men and women who may have very well joined the Order's call. I'm trying to protect you."

"Fine," she grumbled, putting the hat on.

She flipped her long hair out of the hole in the back, and the effect was nothing short of mouthwatering. How she managed to make even a baseball hat sexy, he didn't know.

"Spy mode activated," Raven said, crossing her arms. "Satisfied?"

Not nearly.

Zane knew he would only be satisfied when the Order of Salem was stopped. When Raven agreed to be his mate. When he'd get a chance to make love to her.

Then he'd be satisfied.

He parked the truck and chased after Raven, who hopped out and rushed to the store. When she suddenly stopped, his senses went on high alert.

"What's wrong?" he asked, looking around.

She tipped her head to the side. "See those boys?"

He narrowed his eyes and zeroed in on two older teens slinking around the cars in the lot. One pulled on a door handle, finding the vehicle locked then moved on.

Shit. Just what he needed. Trouble. "Stay here," he said then strode away to come up behind them. Stalking the teens, he listened carefully for their movements. Peeking around a bumper, he studied the boys.

Both wore ragged jeans which he thought could be in style or maybe the only pair they owned. The long-sleeve shirts had threadbare spots and holes. The young ones smelled alike—brothers, each needing a shower.

The older one pulled open a door and unlocked the back side for his brother. They climbed in and searched. With his shifter speed, Zane zipped to the car and closed both doors, trapping the boys inside. The two flipped around to get out, but when seeing Zane, they froze.

One scooted toward the other side and pulled up the post lock. Utilizing his speed again, he "appeared" on the other side of the car and opened the door, scaring the shit out of the kid who screamed and fell over himself to get back.

"Neither of you move," Zane instructed, putting his alpha strength into his words even though the boys were human. The blood drained from both young faces as Zane climbed into the back seat. He sighed and glanced from one expression of terror to the other.

Zane knew what he said or did this moment could change these boys' lives. He had to be careful and be clear.

"Shouldn't you two be in school?" he asked.

The older one narrowed his eyes and sneered his lip. Zane recognized that look as typical defensive posturing taken by those hiding something. In this case, a bad home life? Or maybe a difficult financial situation?

Before the kid had the chance to spout off some snotty reply, Zane frowned at him. "Obviously, you should be. But you're breaking into cars and stealing instead." He held his hand out to the big brother. "Give me your wallet." When the boy hesitated, a growl vibrated from Zane's chest. The boy's eyes widened as he frantically yanked at the back pocket of his jeans.

The teen pulled out an old Velcro billfold and held it out in a shaking hand. Zane opened it, studied the driver's license then handed it back.

"Are you going to call the cops on us?" the younger boy asked.

"No," Zane said. The brothers glanced at

each other. "You both are going to come to the Salem police department on your own—"

"No we're not," the older one said. "Are you crazy?"

Zane smiled and pulled out his wallet badge and flipped it open, revealing his silver Salem star. He almost laughed at the two groans filling the car.

"Not crazy," Zane said, "just busy. I need help at the station. I hope minimum wage is enough to start with." He waited for their reply.

The boys looked at each other again then at him. The little brother asked, "You're going to pay us to do stuff?"

"Of course," he answered. "The child laws are pretty clear cut. But the catch is you will come after school." The boys shared a look, the little one smelling like fear and shame. Why was that? In his mind, he spun through possible reasons, then it dawned on him.

"But first," Zane added, "I need to get you uniforms." He dialed the office on his cell phone. "Hey, Betty, this is Zane. I need your help getting the proper office attire for two boys I just hired as my assistants."

Betty was quiet for a second. "Is this code for

something, Zane? Because I have no idea what the hell you're talking about."

"Yes, it is." Zane didn't want the boys to know he was getting them new clothes to wear to school because the older brother would get embarrassed and not accept "charity." This wasn't charity, the boys would work for him. But he'd seen this type of situation too many times. Now he had a chance to make a difference.

"Boys?" Betty said. "They should be in school, but I bet they're not, hmm."

"You are correct," Zane said.

"Bad home? No money?" she asked.

"I'm thinking both," Zane replied.

"Okay, how old are they?" Zane passed to Betty the info on the driver's license for the older teen and estimated sizes for the younger brother. Arrangements were made to get the clothes to the kids in a few days. Hopefully by then, this Salem Order shit would be over with.

Zane motioned for everyone to get out of the car. "Remember," he said to them, "I know where you live and I *will hunt you down* if you don't show up. Have I made myself clear?" From his wallet, he pulled out a couple one-hundred-dollar bills and handed one to each child. "Get something to eat and whatever else you need."

The brothers stared at the money in his hand, not moving to take it from him. The older one squinted. "Why are you doing this? You don't know shit about us."

Zane grunted. "I know more about you than you think, kid." And none of those things were good. He pushed his hand with the money closer to them. "I don't want to see you stealing anything else or I will put you in jail. Understand?"

The teens nodded, snatched the money from him, and hurried away. Behind him, a woman opened the trunk to the car they had spent the last few minutes in. He gave her a nod and headed for his mate. He hoped like hell she was still there.

Finding her standing in front of a bulletin board, he put a hand on the small of her back to guide her toward the store's entrance, but his palm heated with the touch of her. He couldn't even help himself; he ran a thumb along the curve of her spine.

She looked sideways at him, and he dropped his hand.

"What happened with the boys?" she asked.

He shrugged. "I gave them a job."

"You what?" She stopped and faced him. "Why would you do that?"

"They are kids who need to learn how the world works. You can't always depend on your family to help you." He knew what her family meant to her, so he doubted she'd understand exactly what the boys were experiencing. And if he could help it, she never would.

Before she turned, he saw a grin on her face.

He kept his hands off her as they walked through the aisles, gathering enough food to make a few meals. Everything was fairly normal and domestic. It gave Zane all kinds of ideas as to how it would be to share a life with Raven.

"I need to find something," she said, hurrying off. "I'll be right back." She was around the end of the aisle before he could get in front of the cart he pushed. With a frown, he took off after her with the cart in the lead. He doubted she would find trouble. More than likely, it would find her.

When he turned at the aisle and checked down the next lane, she wasn't there. Her scent spread around him with the current from the air conditioner blowing down. He continued passing row after row toward the far side of the store.

With her absence, his wolf paced. She wouldn't leave the store to get away from him, would she?

He turned the cart around to return to the main part of the store then heard a tiny whimper human ears wouldn't detect. He followed the sound which became more and more of a cry.

In the last aisle, a roll cart loaded with groceries to be shelved had half fallen onto the floor. Candy, gum, and other sugar-laden edibles spread out from one side to another. Under the downed boxes came the sound he'd been following.

Diving into the mess of cardboard and food, Zane threw containers to the side and shoved the cart away to find a toddler lying on the floor with an unopened sucker in her hand.

His wolf didn't pick up the scent of pain from her, just fear. He scooped her out of the boxes, her hand with a death grip on the candy, and checked her over for flesh wounds. Finding none, he breathed a sigh of relief. He lifted her in his arms to sit against his forearm.

"Where's your mommy, little one?" he asked. Her attention was focused on getting the wrapper off the sucker she held. After he peeled the paper off and the sucker was in her mouth, she looked at him. Her sticky hand tapped against his cheek and stuck. When he help her pull away, several whiskers went along for the ride.

He clenched his jaw and rode out the discomfort. He would never underestimate what females felt when waxing their legs...and other parts. His balls sucked up at the thought of each hair down there being ripped out.

He asked about her mother again and she just repeated, "Mommy." Great. Baby talk. One thing he knew nothing about. Pushing his shopping cart with one hand, he retraced his steps.

"Tell me when you see your mommy, okay?" he said.

"Okay," she repeated. He stopped at the end of each row for her to look down, when she wasn't fiddling with her candy. Then he noticed her hair stuck to her hand that had sucker juice on it—along with a few of his whiskers. She couldn't move her arm without pulling her hair. Red stain encircled her pouty lips, dripping down her chin.

She was quickly turning into a gluey disaster. Shit.

The row they just passed was the baby section. He backed them and the cart down the aisle until he reached the baby wipes. He set her in the cart's seat and clicked the straps together that held her in.

Not caring that he hadn't purchased the tube container yet, he popped open the top and pulled out several wet wipes. From there, he cleaned her up, managing to not make more of a mess. When he looked up, he saw Raven at the aisle's end watching him.

Fantastic. She'd never let him live this down. A bachelor caring for a baby. He pushed the cart toward her and stopped next to Raven. On the other side of the store, a commotion started, but he mostly ignored it, thinking up something to say to her.

"Yes," he said before she had the chance to make a snarky comment, "I know how to take care of children." He leaned into her, bringing his mouth to her ear. "I plan on having a large family. Maybe a few pups. Maybe a few spell spinners." He planted a kiss on her neck and smiled at her shiver and the smell of her arousal. Dammit, his cock was awakening.

Her eyes met his for a second then she turned to the babe. "Come here, little one," she said, lifting the child from the cart. "I think I hear your daddy freaking out."

Zane scowled, wondering what she was talking about. From an aisle several down from them, a man slid as if the row had spit him out. He yelled out a name. Terror rolled off the male, his pulse and breathing highly accelerated. The man was definitely freaking out.

The child took the sucker from her mouth, stretched her arm out, and said, "Daddy." Zane let out a whistle, startling the two females with him.

"Sorry," he said, but the goal was achieved. The man looked at them and ran their way. He grabbed the girl from his mate with cries of thank you, thank you. They scuttled away, having their sweet reunion. He and Raven watched.

She asked, "Where did you find her?"

"Aisle seventeen. Tag said one-third off." He grinned when she frowned at him.

"Smart ass." She started to walk away and he followed with the cart.

"I think she pulled a stack of unsteady boxes off a cart trying to get that candy in her mouth. She was stuck underneath."

"Poor thing," Raven said then was quiet for a

moment before saying, "I can't believe I'm telling you this, but I'm impressed, Mr. Badass Sherriff Wolf."

His wolf perked up. It and he wanted to know what they'd done right so they could do it again.

"You seemed to have handled the teens *and* the toddler in stride. No coming unglued or losing your shit. Good job."

His wolf preened under the praise from their mate. Strutting around with his chest puffed up just like Zane wanted to do. He wanted to tell everyone they passed that his mate was impressed with him. Him. Male shifter. Baby cleaner. Teen job giver. He smiled big.

Then Raven bent over and picked up a five-pound bag of salt and dumped it into their cart, he shook his head and pointed at it.

"Hold the phone. Are you hoping to kill me with high blood pressure? Because that's a long-term plan. I'll definitely have a better handle on the Order of Salem before this kills me."

Raven laughed, and the sound of it made him feel lighter.

"Don't be silly. If I wanted to kill you, I would have turned you into a toad days ago. This," she gestured to the salt, "is for magic. I need it to work some spells."

"No," Zane tried to pick up the bag, but Raven put a hand on his arm.

"I need it, Zane. You might not want me to do magic at the cabin. I don't understand why, but there you have it. But I need this salt. I need it to feel safe and secure."

He knew that she was purposefully cryptic about the use the salt would have, but a busy supermarket was definitcly not the place to have this conversation.

If the salt was going to help Raven feel at ease in his cabin, then she could have the damn thing. But there was still not a chance in hell that she was going to do magic. Zane wasn't sure how, but he knew the Order of Salem could track magic. It sat like a bad feeling in the pit of his stomach every time he thought about it.

Zane began pushing the cart, effectively ending their discussion about the salt.

"Thank you," Raven whispered, following down the aisle.

Don't thank me yet, love.

CHAPTER TWENTY-TWO

ZANE

Raven stood by the stove in Zane's cabin. She stirred the spaghetti sauce, humming softly to herself, swaying to the sound of the music she had insisted they put on. He couldn't remember the last time music had played in his house, but he would make sure to have a radio on hand at all times from now on.

Zane leaned on the counter and watched Raven for a few moments. She was swaying her hips to the music, mouthing the words. It was nice that she was there. And really, if he was being honest about it, he was already planning their next visit up to the cabin.

Next time, there would be no witch hunters after them. It would be an escapade of the romantic variety, and clothing would be entirely optional.

Zane could only hope things would progress that way with his mate. He was already feeling his heart inflating with love for her, a woman he barely knew, but one that was most definitely his mate. His desire for her thrummed just under his skin, making his wolf aware that their woman was right there. Within arms' reach.

It took Zane a few seconds to realize Raven was staring back at him.

"You're giving me that look," she whispered. Her eyes were hooded, yet they burned brighter than Zane had ever noticed before.

"What look?" he asked, his own voice quiet.

"The one that got us into some trouble last night. And then again this morning."

Zane took a step back, raising his hands up in defeat.

"You're right. And I promised I wouldn't touch you. My apologies, Raven."

He turned out of the kitchen and set the silverware and parm cheese for their meal. He could feel Raven's eyes on him as he moved around, but he couldn't figure out why. Every time he chanced a glance at her, her face was blank, leaving him no clue.

He hoped she was giving his words from earlier some thought.

There would be no more kissing, no more touching, until she came to him. It wasn't an ultimatum. It was more like an incentive. He knew it was only a matter of time before Raven realized they were good together and that he was nothing like her ex.

Zane hadn't realized just how difficult it would be for him to keep away from her. It wasn't just the close proximity in the small cabin.

"It's ready," Raven said, getting two plates from the cabinet.

Zane walked around her, getting the garlic bread out of the oven. The smell of the garlic butter, typically one of his favorite scents, seemed dull to him. And all because Raven was standing right there. She was his favorite odor.

They settled at the table and ate in silence. The air felt heavy, though. There were unsaid things hanging between them.

"The quiet is driving me crazy," Raven said, dropping her fork on the table. "Talk to me."

Zane was completely stunned by her words,

and he slowly put down his own fork, swallowing his bite, not knowing how to respond.

"Well, all right. What should we talk about?"

"I don't know." She shrugged. "But you say I'm your mate and you don't know anything about me. Aren't there things you want to know?"

He thought about this for a few seconds. Were there?

"I know you're a strong, intelligent, capable woman. I know you love your family and run a successful business. I also know that you're kind and caring. Sure, you're a bit stubborn, but I feel like I know what I need to."

Raven rolled her eyes at him. "I don't know anything about you. I mean, I know you're the sheriff and the beta in your pack, but that's it."

This irked him a bit. Hadn't she seen some of his qualities over their short time together? Perhaps getting Raven to agree to be his mate would be more difficult than he thought.

And he was thinking it would be almost impossible.

So there was that.

"Ask me whatever you want to know," he said.

Raven leaned her elbows on the table and

cupped her cheeks. Her eyes were on him, brow furrowed.

Shit.

She looked like she was about to ask him some tough questions.

"Do you have any siblings?" she asked.

That wasn't so bad. He couldn't help but wonder if she was working her way up to the difficult stuff.

"No," he answered, taking a sip of his beer. "I've always been close to Axel."

"I can't even imagine that. Cerise and I have always been glued at the hip. On top of that, our cousins, Astra and Selene, are our age, too. So it was the two sets of twins causing trouble from jump."

"I'm sorry, did you just say that your cousins are twins also?"

"Yup," Raven wiggled her eyebrows at him. "Twins are a thing in the Bishop family. For real. My mother is a twin. Auntie Edith is older than mom by all of two minutes. It was cool growing up surrounded by family, though. My parents are pretty inseparable from my aunt and uncle. They moved to California a little while ago. Now they're doing this insane cruise around the world."

"That sounds like a fun adventure for them."

Zane loved Raven's smile, and there it was, lighting up her entire face as she thought about her family.

"It is. I'm also very happy they're nowhere near Salem right now. I wouldn't want to have to worry about them. Even if they would have more knowledge on offensive magic. I don't want them to get involved and possibly get hurt."

"We'll figure it all out," he said.

He didn't even notice that his hand had reached out for hers. He gave it a squeeze and let go. Raven looked away, sighing deeply.

"I'm not used to going through things alone. Usually, I have my girls there with me."

"You're not alone, Raven. I'm here. And even if Cerise is far away with Axel, even if your cousins are hiding out with other wolves, you're all in this together."

"It's not the same. We'd be lying on one of our beds, making plans, and practicing spells to make sure we could win over these mother fuckers."

It was on the tip of his tongue to tell her that

they could also lie on the bed and make plans. Of course, he didn't say those words to her. Because of his earlier promise. And because there would be nothing innocent happening once he got Raven on a bed.

She pushed back her plate, having barely eaten anything. That didn't sit too well with Zane. He didn't like seeing his mate so torn up about being apart from her kin. And he definitely didn't like the fact there were people out to get her.

"Why don't you go relax. Sit by the fire and take it easy. I'll do the cleanup."

"Not a chance," she said, grabbing her plate and taking it to the kitchen sink. "If I just sit there, I'll go crazy. I need to do something to keep my mind off everything."

"Fine," he shrugged, following her into the kitchen. "But I'll wash, you dry."

"Deal."

They were back to working in silence, but Zane wanted to keep talking with her. Not only did he like the sound of her voice, but also the way talking with her made him breathe easier. It soothed him and his wolf. The damn animal was all kinds of loud and obnoxious in his head. He would not press her against the counter and take her right there. Nope.

"Umm…so what kind of witch are you?"

He knew the answer, but he had to do something to keep from imagining what it would be like to lick his way across Raven's pussy. It was getting harder to ignore the wolf.

Especially since Raven was right there, and their hands kept brushing as he passed her clean dishes for her to dry.

"I'm an air witch. So that means I can control air. Cerise is earth. Astra is fire and Selene water, so when we were kids, we got into some shit."

"Um, why?"

"Well, there are four elements. Each of us has a different power. We did some spells we really shouldn't have. Cerise and Astra were the worst for that. They would find these ancient spells and make us do them. We accidentally burned down a shed. And we also almost caused an international incident."

His brow furrowed. "How?"

"Oh, you're a cop. And I really don't know if the statute of limitations is past yet. I plead the fifth."

"Not exactly how that works, but fine. Keep

your secrets. But for what it's worth, I think that pushing the limits of our powers is just what supernatural kids do. I mean, Axel and I got into some shit when were pups. I took the fall a lot because Axel was the future alpha. The adults would have been even harder on him than they were on me."

"Somehow, I can't imagine you breaking any rules. Especially not now. You're the sheriff. You're all about the rules."

Raven bumped her hip against him playfully.

It was innocent teasing, but it was too much for Zane.

In a flash, he had her up against the counter, hands cupping her face, mouth sealed to hers.

He didn't think, he just acted on pure instinct. Raven was his mate, and she was there with him. She had brushed her body against his, and he had come alive. Awareness sparking in his cock, his heart, his head.

As he devoured her mouth with passion, his wolf howled loudly.

Mine.

CHAPTER TWENTY-THREE

RAVEN

Kissing Zane in the small, cramped kitchen of the secluded cabin shouldn't have been Raven's most sensual moment or her best kiss ever. But it was. As Zane kissed her, making her feel like the sexiest woman in existence, all Raven could do was hold on for dear life and kiss him back.

With every movement of his lips against hers, Raven melted more and more.

Oh.

Oh, wow.

That's all Raven could formulate as thoughts. Zane's kisses were banishing any logic she could have. She couldn't think to push him away.

She didn't want to.

She wanted to keep kissing Zane until her lips fell off. Because the man could kiss, and the way he moved his lips against hers, the way his tongue plundered her mouth was too good.

It was primal; she could feel that.

But there was something else mixed in. Desperation, maybe. Yup. Zane, hot sheriff and wolf shifter, was desperate for her. It was a powerful thing to realize.

She moaned and threaded her fingers in his hair, needing him to be closer.

It was then that Zane pulled away from her.

"Fuck, Raven. I am so sorry."

He turned and ran his hands through his hair a couple of times, his breathing coming out in pants.

"Why?" she asked, genuinely confused by his sudden dismissal of her kisses. Wasn't this what he had been wanting? For her to be responsive to his advances?

"I shouldn't have done that."

"Well, in case you didn't notice, I was totally into it until you stopped."

Zane turned to face her, confusion on his handsome face.

"Yeah, I know, but…"

"Shit, Zane. What am I going to do with you?"

Raven was asking herself that question more than she was him. What the actual fuck was she doing?

Here was this man, a good man, one who was caring and sweet in his own way. He was telling her that she was his. And she was pushing him away?

And why? Because some asshole had broken her spirit? Her emotions were all over the place and her brain took a moment to tell her to trust this. Why? Because Arthur had fucked with her mind. He'd made her retreat into herself and build enough walls she'd never get hurt again. But what if Zane wasn't going to hurt her. What if they could build something special, together. This was her chance to find out. Her chest squeezed. Fear had kept her from trying to do anything with anyone else.

Here was Zane being a good guy and she was being a total bitch to him. He didn't deserve that. He'd been sweet and kind and so damn good at kissing. She had to stop torturing him with her attitude and torturing herself by denying what could be something amazing between them.

She was a Bishop witch, for fuck's sake. She had moped around long enough about Arthur. He had stolen years from her life. She wasn't going to let her hurt dictate her future anymore.

If anything, the fact that Zane was being so respectful to her wish for space was a huge selling point as to the kind of man he was. Yes, he kept slipping up and kissing her despite the promise he had made, but that was how much he wanted her. It made her feel powerful to be so desirable, so irresistible to him.

Arthur had been a jerk with a verbally abusive streak.

Zane was the polar opposite. There he was, a hot man standing in front of her, ready to give her things she didn't quite understand. He wanted to protect her, even when said protection drove her insane. He didn't see her magic as a personality flaw like Arthur had. Yes, Zane didn't want her to use her power. Not because he hated that she was a witch, but because he was scared for her. That was a new sort of emotion for Raven.

No one, outside of her family, had ever cared for her wellbeing.

She watched as Zane went back to work on the dishes.

She wanted to give in.

Raven really wanted to see what it would be like to be loved by a man like Zane, a shifter who had loyalty running through his veins. Love. Loyalty. She'd wanted that all her life and never thought she'd get it after Arthur.

There was no going back once she opened that door. Once they were together, that would be it. She wouldn't be able to hide behind her fear or her ire at being locked away from the world.

Could she deal with that?

She was already fighting one battle with the Order of Salem. She couldn't fight with herself on top of that. Not anymore.

Raven took a few steps toward Zane, and she closed her arms around his waist. Before he could even react, she dropped a kiss onto his parted lips. She made sure to run her tongue along the seam of his mouth in a teasing caress.

"What are you doing?" Zane asked, his voice breaking on the words.

"Isn't it obvious?" she answered, kissing the side of his mouth.

"Raven," he warned.

"Wait," she cleared her throat. "Before you say anything. I need to apologize."

He frowned. "What? Why?"

"I've been a total bitch to you from the first moment you came into my shop." She licked her lips and let her shoulders drop. "I argued every step of the way and even knowing it was unnecessary, I still continued. Even when I knew you were right and things were for my safety, I argued. I'm sorry."

"You don't have to apologize for being cautious."

She shook her head. "It's more than caution. I...I had a bad break-up. That ex I told you about, the asshole. Arthur... he destroyed my sense of self. I didn't want to allow any other man to make me question who I am. Make me feel I'm not good enough because of who I am. Or how I look" She met glanced at his too sexy lips. "I've made your job harder. I've been a total jerk and you don't deserve it." She glanced down at his jaw. "I told myself I would never allow any man to talk down to me. To belittle me. But I've been the one who's been a hormonal bitch and it's totally uncalled for." She met his gaze. "I promise to be more receptive to your advice and stop being such a mean-spirited bitch."

He grinned. "Baby, you're a strong woman. I

understand past situations have made you mistrust men and people in general. I want you as you are, Raven. I accept you exactly as you come. Curves, attitude and all."

She sucked in a breath and kissed his lips. His words warmed her from the inside and calmed the racing fear around her heart. She didn't even build the embrace, she dipped her tongue into his mouth and locked her arms around his neck.

Zane growled, cupping her ass, making sure all of their parts were lining up just right. Lips moved against lips, tongues explored, teeth clanked as they went at each other with the passion of two starved people.

He pulled away after a few moments.

"Are you sure?" he asked, placing a large hand over her heart. His question was about so much more than the moment they were about to share.

Raven nodded, but Zane licked his lips, still keeping his distance.

"Isn't this what you wanted?" she asked. "Me coming at you willingly? Because this is exactly what this is."

"I don't think you understand what this would mean for me. For you. Once I get a taste of you, there is no going back, Raven."

"So come and taste me," she purred.

Raven was surprised by the wanton sound of her voice, by the way she was asking for exactly what she wanted. She'd never done that before, and now that she knew what it felt like for Zane to look at her like he wanted to eat her whole, she knew she'd make more of her needs known.

Zane cupped her ass and lifted her. She closed her legs around his waist, and with his long, powerful legs, he took them to the small bedroom. His eyes didn't leave hers as he gently lay her on the bed.

He had barely touched her yet, but Raven already knew.

This was going to be the best.

CHAPTER TWENTY-FOUR

RAVEN

Raven laid down on Zane's bed, and she watched as he took his shirt off. She'd seen him naked twice already, but she couldn't help but to feast her eyes on the absolute spectacle his upper body was. Zane was a wall of muscles, rippling abs, wide shoulders, and strong arms.

She couldn't wait to see the rest of him, but he surprised the hell out of her by kneeling down between her legs on the bed. Zane slowly unzipped her jeans and flicked the button. He was being so fucking slow about it, Raven was sure he was trying to make her go crazy.

"You could hurry it up, you know," she grunted.

"Not a chance, love. I am taking my time with you tonight. I am going to strip you bare and then make you come so many times, you won't remember any other man."

Raven inhaled sharply. She wanted to gripe about how possessive that was, but she couldn't find it in her to actually want anything else. If Zane was offering her a brand-new set of experiences that could erase years of bad sex with Arthur, then so be it.

He threw the pants over his shoulder and gently tugged down her underwear. Raven sent out a silent prayer to Cerise, who was always on her case about personal grooming. Zane's appreciative groan was all the thanks she needed for waxing her bikini line regularly.

Zane spread her legs wide and inhaled her scent.

"You're so pretty and pink," he whispered before dropping a kiss straight onto her clit.

Raven hadn't been ready for the touch, and she bucked off the bed as his lips grazed the tight bundle of nerves.

"Oh, you liked that, beautiful?" he asked, his voice rough and low.

She didn't have time to answer. He kissed her sex again, this time adding his tongue to the mix.

"I wanted to take my time, but here I am, rushing. You're not even naked."

He helped her out of her shirt and unhooked her bra. His eyes went round as he freed her aching globes. He cupped each one in a large hand and ran his thumb across her sensitive nipples.

"You know, I can smell your desire, Raven. I can tell just how much you want me."

Zane dipped down and took one of her nipples into his mouth as his other hand tweaked the other nub. He kissed his way to her other breast and showed that one the same attention. Raven was a panting mess under him, lifting her legs off the bed, looking for some kind of pressure against her core.

"You're being very impatient," he whispered against her skin, making her shiver.

"You're the one who wants to take it slow. I didn't say I was on board for that."

"Hush," he murmured, nuzzling his way down to her pussy.

He placed on hand on each of her thighs, and he kissed the inside of each knee, trailing more kisses down the length of each leg. With every drop of his lips against her heated skin, Raven bucked off the bed, searching for more.

When he finally settled his mouth on her clit, she was all but thrashing on the bed, begging for an orgasm. She'd never been so turned on, so desperate to come. Zane had made her into nothing but a puddle of want and desire.

Though he had said he wanted to take his time, he wasted none bringing her to the edge of pleasure. His tongue twirled around the hood of her clit, and he took to suckling it. It was all too much for Raven after all of the teasing. One of his thick fingers traced her entrance, never actually making it in. The teasing of it was intense, and she ground her pussy against his face shamelessly. She chased down the orgasm like it was the only thing keeping her alive.

The tingles of her climax weren't soft as they raced her to release. She cried out Zane's name, and he chuckled against her sex as he kept licking her, savoring the aftershocks of her completion.

"You're wild when you come, love. I want to see that again when you're full of my dick."

"Yes," she moaned, already craving more of everything Zane had to offer.

He kicked off his jeans and his boxers. His thick erection stood proudly between his legs, making Raven blush. It was by far the biggest, most beautiful penis she had ever seen. Could dicks even be beautiful? This one definitely was. Probably only because it was Zane's.

"How do you want to do this?" he asked her.

For a few seconds, her brain lagged, and she wasn't sure what he meant.

"Bare."

His eyes widened. "Are you-"

"I'm sure," Raven answered. She'd never had sex without the thin layer of latex, but if it was going to happen in her life, it would be tonight. With that man, who she trusted so completely, even after such a short time.

He gave her a crooked smile. "Thank fuck." His voice was nothing but a rumbling growl. "I don't want anything between us. I want to feel all of your smooth velvety grip around my dick."

His eyes looked deep inside hers as he took the solid column of his cock in his hand. Raven watched, half in expectation, half in fascination as he lined himself up with her center. He eased in slowly. He never looked away from her, and when he tapped out, something clicked between them. Raven felt it deep in her soul and shivered.

"Move," she begged, needing to get away from the pure admiration she saw in his eyes.

He did, his thrusts in and out a slow, torturous affair. Raven took hold of his muscular shoulder and held on as Zane worked on building another orgasm deep inside her core. She clenched the walls of her pussy around the thick length, desperately trying to keep him within her. She needed him, all of him.

"Fuck, Zane," she cried out just before the orgasm hit.

It was a wall of pleasure that she crashed into, over and over again. She knew she was calling out his name, gripping his back tightly. Above her, Zane was caught between triumphant and loving. It was an odd sort of mix, but it was a good look on him.

It made Raven glow from the inside out. Not just from the orgasm, but from feeling like this was exactly where she needed to be.

In Zane's arms.

His own climax was a loud roar as he emptied himself inside her. He was motionless above her, panting for a few seconds, before dropping a kiss on her shoulder and rolling onto his back.

"That was…" his voice was raspy. She heard him swallow and sat up to give him a wink.

"The end of that sentence better be good, because that was fucking phenomenal for me."

"Oh, love. It definitely was just that and so much more."

It only took them a few moments to clean up, and they were back in the bed together.

Zane lay on his side, and Raven nuzzled into him, loving the feel of his warm, muscular skin against her own. It was blissful to be in his arms. She inhaled their scent and let it lull her into a sense of peace.

"I wasn't expecting that to happen," she said, letting her fingers trail along his abdomen.

"No? I was definitely hoping this would happen."

He chuckled, making her entire body vibrate. She pinched his side. "More than that," she said. "You were actively seducing me."

"Was not," he argued. "I promised to stay away. And I was able to."

"What? How? By constantly brushing up

against me? By being sweet and thoughtful? No, you knew what you were doing, Sheriff Devious."

"I can't help it, Raven. You're mine, and I feel it profoundly. I'm always going to try to make you happy.

"It's okay," she sighed happily. "I guess I was kind of playing the same game."

"You mean like dancing in the kitchen?"

She balked. "I always dance when I'm cooking."

"And you always should. It was a lovely sight."

She rolled her eyes, but it was at odds with the giggle that escaped her. Zane's fingers drew patterns along her back, making her sigh contently.

"I'm sleepy," she whispered against his chest.

"Then rest, love."

He maneuvered them, pasting his front to her back, an arm holding her close to him around her waist.

He wasn't going to let her go. Not now, not ever.

Something had changed between them, and he was definitely not going to let Raven regret this night.

"Goodnight, love," he whispered softly.

"Night," she murmured, inching back toward him.

Raven fell asleep in Zane's arms, knowing she had never been so safe. In the depths of her chest, her heart took on the same beat as his, and a different kind of magic was at work.

CHAPTER TWENTY-FIVE

ZANE

Zane couldn't quite believe his luck. Not only had they spent the better part of the night worshiping each other's bodies. They'd woken up sometime in the middle of the night and made love again.

That was the only way Zane could classify it. It had been a slow, unhurried affair. It had been so intense, Raven had come all over his dick twice. He would never get tired of the way she came. Her entire body flushed, and her pussy clamped down on him as if they were two pieces that should never be separated.

The night's crowning moment was when Raven had fallen asleep in his arms. There was something sweet about it, and the way she curled up against his side like she could never be close enough.

Now, as the morning light streamed in from the blinds, Zane was starting off his day with his mate still wrapped up in him. Her dark hair was sprawled on his chest, and he could hear her deep, restful breathing. He wanted to run his hands through her black curls, but he didn't want to wake her.

He wanted to relish this time they had together. Raven had come to him.

She had given herself to him, and she'd spent the night in his bed. The fact she was still next to him was encouraging. It might be a small, unconscious gesture, but it meant everything to him. It took the hope he had and built on it.

He knew that something had changed between them during their special night together.

He wasn't just her protector anymore. He was well on his way to being her man. The person she could rely on when shit went sideways. The one she'd spend her life with. He could feel it in his soul, and judging by the way his big bad wolf was purring deep inside him, he knew everything would be all right.

"Morning," she breathed, leaning up on an

elbow. She dropped a quick peck on his lips before rushing out of bed.

He watched her ass as she ran to the bathroom. The shower kicked on, and he chuckled. He had no doubt she would empty the hot water tank while she washed her long, thick hair. He made a mental note that he would have to upgrade the tanks at his place and at the cabin so that Raven could have all of the hot water she needed while he didn't have to contend with cold showers.

He didn't intend to take any of those. Not now that he and Raven were together.

Though they hadn't explicitly stated the words during their sexcapade, Zane had warned her that once she came to him, that would be it. They would be together.

Zane rolled out of bed and made his way to the kitchen where he got coffee and breakfast ready for them. If he was lucky, Raven would be up for another round once she got done with her primping. He was just pouring milk into his cereal when Raven walked out of the bathroom, wrapping a towel around her long, black tresses.

"I think we should go back to Salem," Raven said.

Zane's heart stopped.

So much for thinking they had made headway during their night together. Those words were truly the last ones he expected to hear.

"What? No. We can't. We're still waiting on word from the pack and the station to see what they've discovered."

"I don't want to keep waiting here. As great as it's been, being shacked up here with you, I kind of got caught up in you and me. I should be out there with Cerise, with my cousins."

Zane crossed his arms, ready to rebuke her, but Raven wasn't done.

"To top it all off, I have a house to fix and a business to run. Cerise and I are the only staff, so if we aren't there to open the store, we aren't making any money. We can't afford that. We can go back to Salem, and you can protect me from there."

He blew out a huge breath and shook his head. "Do you think I have the resources to follow you around Salem?"

"Well, you seem to have the resources to keep four very capable witches in separate locations, so I don't see what the big deal is with this."

"Raven, after last night, I thought…"

Confusion flashed in her eyes. "Don't you dare," she growled like the proper wolf mate she was. "If you open that talented mouth of yours to tell me that you expect me to follow all your plans and ideas after we had sex a couple of times…"

He couldn't help but hiss. Her words had felt like a slap against his cheeks. She blushed and bit down on her lips.

"That came out wrong. Sorry. I just…" She sighed heavily. "Look, while I was in the shower, I was thinking, and it kind of cleared my head. We can't hide forever. An attack on the Order of Salem would be best. We won't wait around to be picked off one by one like our ancestors did all those years ago. I want to be on the offense."

Zane opened his mouth to argue with her, but Raven wasn't even close to being done.

"If we attack them, we end them. Then that's it. No more hiding. No more ban on magic. We can go about our lives as before. I have the perfect idea. My magic is back up and running after the fight, so here's what we do."

Raven sat at the table in front of him. He was reluctant to say anything. He didn't trust his words would be very nice. "I call Cerise and we get my cousins in on it, too. We do a locator spell and we find each member of the Order of Salem and send one of your officers to arrest them. That way, you aren't breaking any sheriff rules and we are home free.

"And though that would be a spell that might deplete our magic for a bit, it shouldn't be that hard if we all get together. Besides, the chances are that a lot of the members of the Order will be together."

Zane sighed.

Fuck. That was actually a decent plan.

Or it would have been if he didn't suspect that the Order of Salem could track magic somehow.

"Let's say we do this. We get all four of you Bishops together, and you do the spell. We locate all of them. The second they sense magic, they will be on us."

"But we would have the pack and your cops, right?"

"Raven, you asking me to put the men and women of my station against a deranged order? We don't know how many there are, what kinds of weapons they have. I can't, in good conscience, ask anyone to walk into that fight with me. Besides, if we shifters had to turn into our wolves, how would we explain that to the other officers?"

"Okay, so it might not be the best plan," she responded, deflated by his words. "But we could still be four witches and a wolf."

"We would be four witches and four wolves," Zane corrected. "And we have no idea how much magic you all would have after the locating spell. So in actuality, it would be four wolves against however many members the order has."

"Fine. It was a bad, shitty plan. And I am a horrible person for thinking that other people would walk into a fight, risking their lives with very little information."

Zane sighed and reached across the table, taking her hand in his. "It's not a shitty idea, Raven. And asking that doesn't make you a bad person. You've just never had to fight a life and death battle before. And that's a good thing."

"All of this would work, you know. Four witches and four wolves, because I am telling you. The only way for the Order of Salem to track magic is to have magic. And they are clearly against the idea, so we would be in the clear."

"We don't know that for sure," he sighed again, felling his lungs burning with the force of it. It didn't help that she looked so completely dejected by his rebuttal of her plan. "And I won't take a chance with your life or your family's lives. Do you understand?"

"Well, we can't just sit here anymore, doing nothing. I had the best night of my life last night, and that makes me feel like absolute shit because I don't know how Cerise is, and I have no idea where Astra and Selene are. So we need to get moving with something so I can stop feeling so goddamn shitty for being happy."

Zane blinked rapidly, trying to make sense of the spitfire words Raven had just shot out at him.

She was happy after the best night of her life?

That was encouraging.

"Love, we will find a plan. One that will keep magic and shifters separate from the human world, and one that will see the end of the Order. But let's agree that doing magic is dangerous right now."

"It's not. Magic is part of who I am."

"I know, Raven. And it really kills me that I have to tell you not to do something that is such an integral part of who you are. But it's for your safety, I swear."

Raven sat back in her chair, blowing out a hot breath and crossing her arms over her chest.

"I don't think this is the right way of doing things. I should be using my strengths."

"How about this… You let me try to come up with a plan before we use magic, all right?"

"If I had my phone, I would be able to do some research on magic." She gave him a pointed look, and Zane understood exactly what she was saying.

Raven was giving him a stare down to rival all stare downs he had ever done. And he interrogated criminals for a living. She could give him a run for his money.

"Here's what we will do… I have a few calls to make to the station. I need to check how things are there, and I also need to do another perimeter check. I'll check in with Axel and see what we can do."

"A witch and a wolf should be enough to defend each other."

"Raven," he breathed, shaking his head. "It's not. That isn't to say you're not a powerful witch, but we have no idea what we are up against. Let me work my own kind of magic first, all right?"

"Fine," she answered with an attitude that indicated that everything was anything but fine. It was a sharp tone that irked him. He hated that they were already fighting. Their bliss had been short-lived.

His mate had finally given in to their mutual attraction. Instead of running around his property in wolf form, he had been busy making Raven achieve multiple orgasms. That was a priority, but so should be her safety.

Zane dropped his phone onto the porch, stripped out of his clothes and shifted into his wolf

How they had gone from having the best night of her life to being so at odds with each other was beyond him. Zane didn't know how, but he knew he had to fix this, and fast.

Raven was right. They couldn't play house and hide anymore.

They had to fight their way out of this.

CHAPTER TWENTY-SIX

RAVEN

From inside of the cabin, Raven watched as Zane shifted into his wolf shape. Though she had seen him shift a couple of times now, she still couldn't wrap her mind around how cool it was to see him transforming into an animal.

The gray wolf ran toward the forest lining the property and disappeared.

This is my chance.

Raven didn't know much about law enforcement or the minds of criminals and lunatic psychos who wanted to kill a bunch of people for being just who they were.

But she knew magic. It had been a part of her since birth. And she didn't believe it could be used against her. She would use magic, and she would prove to Zane he was wrong. They'd be home free in no time at all.

Sneaking on the tips of her toes to the cupboard where they had put the salt, Raven kept looking over her shoulder. She didn't know how long she had, but she had to be quick and efficient so Zane didn't catch her in the act.

He'd be pissed, which she could deal with.

But he'd also stop her, and she wasn't having any of that.

They'd had sex. The best sex of her life, actually. But that didn't make her any less a witch or any less competent to take care of herself and her people. Even if she was now willing to accept his help. Without the attitude. She still could do things to protect them.

Raven took the huge bag of salt she'd purchased in town.

She knew what had to be done. If she was quick about it, she could put protective wards around the house, and then she could do all the magic she wanted within the walls of the cabin. The Order of Salem wouldn't be able to track her. The issue was that if they were already looking for magic, then the spell to ward the house would give them the location.

It was a chance she would have to take.

Besides, her magic was completely replenished, and she knew how to make sure she didn't deplete it so quickly this time around. She shouldn't make the biggest airball she could. That took too much energy, and then to throw it was even more of a drain on her. She had to make a bunch of small ones and throw them.

Raven also had this wild idea that maybe she could shove air at the psychos from the order. She hadn't tried it yet, but as soon as she had the wards up, she was going to try.

She didn't necessarily believe that the order could track her magic like Zane feared. But if—on the off chance they could—she'd rather be able to tell Zane she had been doing it to protect them.

Not that she was practicing her offensive magic.

Either way, he'd get all growly at her. Raven didn't particularly like the fact she was concerned about his emotions, but she was starting to feel things for the guy. She couldn't help it.

It wasn't just because the sex had been good.

Well, better than good. Fucking amazing, if she was honest with herself.

But Zane was actually a really sweet guy when he wasn't stomping around like an annoyed wolf. The way he handled the kids at the store surprised her. She thought for sure he would have put the boys in jail, but instead, he gave them a second chance. Then watching him clean up the little girl—he had no fear, knew exactly what to do. At least he wouldn't be a clueless father.

Raven placed the salt on the kitchen counter, and she could have sworn the weight of it made the table's legs buckle. She placed her two hands, palms down, over the salt. She knew this spell well. It was one of the first she had been taught as a young witch.

With her eyes closed, she reached deep within herself. Her magic was there. She pulled at it like a thread, and it rushed around inside her veins. She spoke a witch's blessing over the salt. Just like the incantation called for, she repeated the words twice more.

This spell worked better if it was done on the night of a full moon, but midday sun would have to do. She grabbed the salt and exited the cabin through the front door. At the bottom of the two steps, Raven cleared her mind and tipped the salt bag. A small pile of white crystals fell onto the ground, and she could sense the magic building in the air. If the order could track her magic, she hoped this magical pulse wasn't enough to get their attention.

Keeping her pace steady, yet slow enough to be respectful of the element she was calling to work the ward magic, she walked the perimeter of the cabin three times. Once to banish all negative energies, a second to purify the space, and a third to protect it.

It was the third go that took it out of her. Usually, when she did this spell, she had Cerise with her. Together, they were a powerful force, but without her twin, it was like she only had access to half her magic. The air around her was shaking from the magic pulsing through it.

She closed the third circle back at the bottom of the stairs and took a few steps back to admire her handiwork. If the Order of Salem came, then so be it.

Now, with the circle complete, she could go back inside and contact Cerise through astral projection. Sure, that would put a bit of a damper on her magic, but it would be worth it. It was too bad Zane had thrown her phone away. She could have used it to call Cerise instead of using the magic airways.

But just as Raven was about to walk up the steps and into the cabin, she heard trees rustling.

"What did you do?" Zane asked, stalking toward her as naked as the day he was born.

Raven tucked the empty salt bag behind her back. She didn't know why she was trying to hide it. He'd see it for sure. More than that, the man had bought the salt for her. He couldn't be surprised she had actually used it.

"What do you mean?" she shot back, playing the innocent.

"You did something. I was out running the property, and I felt something in the air. A shift of some kind. The air got tighter. What did you do?"

"I put up wards around the cabin. Now I can do magic from inside the space, and the Order of Salem won't be able to track us."

"Oh?" he crossed his arms, fury shooting out of his green eyes. "And what about the magic you just performed to get the wards up? Don't you think they felt that?"

"I used very little power, Zane," she said. "I doubt they could feel it even if the order was capable of tracking magic. But like I told you, they would need their own magic wielder to be able to tell when we do magic. I'm not too worried."

"Yeah, well, you should be."

"I am the witch here, right? So I should theoretically know more about magic, right?"

"Yes, love." There was nothing loving about his tone. "But I'm the sheriff, right? So I definitely know more about criminals and how they work. And I can guarantee you that if they're coming after witches now, it's because they feel like they have an edge. That edge can't be guns. Those are too easy to get in this country."

"You didn't leave me much of a choice, Zane. You put your foot down, and what? I was just supposed to listen to you because you're the man? Because you have the badge?"

"No, Raven. You should listen because you trust me. But it's clear you don't. Not after this stunt. I get that your ex hurt you, but you should have trusted me to make the right call on this."

Zane bound up the stairs and walked into the cabin. Raven chased after him.

"Oh, no, you don't. I didn't tell you about

Arthur so you could throw it in my face. He has nothing to do with this."

"Doesn't he?" Zane asked, putting his pants back on. "You're telling me he was one-hundred-percent all right with you being a witch? That when I told you that you shouldn't use magic, you decided to do it anyway because you thought I was saying it was a bad thing?"

Raven crossed her arms and bit down on her lips. He was right. That was exactly what had her reacting so strongly to the fact she couldn't use magic. It had completely blinded her to the words that Zane had told her about the dangers of using magic.

The realization made her entire body ache.

She had fucked up. She could only hope that Zane was wrong. That the Order of Salem couldn't track magic.

"Shit. I'm sorry," Raven shook her head. "I keep thinking he didn't do any damage. That I got out of it scot-free. I'm…sorry."

"You don't apologize for having a past. Or for having scars because of it. That's not why I'm saying these things to you, Raven. I didn't think that telling you not to do magic was so tied to your heartache. I should have seen it."

"Arthur and I were together for a long time. He was never okay with the fact I was a witch. It bugged him, and he accused me of using it against him a bunch of times. I could only really practice when I was at Gemstones or with Cerise and my cousins. I didn't think it had left such an impression. I really thought you were telling me to not use magic because you don't trust me."

"No, of course, I trust you. But like I said, we have no idea what we are up against. That's the only reason why I said it was a bad idea."

She bit her lip. "I wasn't hearing that. My perception of your words was really twisted." She winced. "I'm sorry I keep doing that."

Zane nodded and sighed. "Are you sure you're ready for this?"

For a few seconds, Raven thought he meant the fight they would have to rage against the Order, but when he pointed to each of them, it was clear what he meant.

She swallowed hard and allowed determination to steel her spine. "Yes, I'm sure. I just have to work on hearing what you're saying instead of putting my own twist on it. It won't happen right away, but I promise to not judge anything you say based on the past. You've shown me you're nothing like Arthur and I will remind myself often of that."

"I'll make sure to be clear as well, so there's no misunderstandings. And, Raven? I would never ask you to be ashamed of you who are, of what you are capable of. I'm a shifter. If anyone can understand power and the intricacies of it, it's me."

This man was going to make her weak at the knees. Raven opened her mouth to respond to his sweet comment, but the words died when the entire ground rumbled beneath her feet. She gasped, holding onto the table.

"What's wrong?" Zane asked, rushing toward her.

"Didn't you feel that earthquake?" she asked, still feeling the ground under her feet trembling.

Zane furrowed his brow. "What earthquake?"

"You're not feeling the ground shake?" Her voice was quaking and her heart turned cold when Zane shook his head.

"Then, that can only mean one thing. Someone has just used magic in a very big way. And since I felt it, it was someone I'm close to. Cerise."

Zane rushed to his phone.

"You need to call Axel," she said, feeling her limbs heavy at her side with panic.

"Already on it."

Even at a small distance, Raven could hear the phone ring and ring, but no one picked up.

"What kind of spell do you think she could have done to make the ground shake so much?"

"I don't know… How far are they?"

Zane shook his head. "Don't be mad… They're across the lake. Barely twenty minutes."

"Well, shit. Had I known, I would have swum to get to her."

"One thing is for sure," Zane said with a shake of his head, "if the Order of Salem can track your magic, that just sent them to Cerise and Axel in a big way."

CHAPTER TWENTY-SEVEN

RAVEN

Raven stood in the kitchen, waiting to feel the ground shake again, but there was nothing. She didn't dare pace. She was scared she'd feel more magic thrumming underfoot. Something was irking her.

How had Cerise been able to do so much magic all by herself? Her twin's power was on par with her, and it seemed to Raven like there had been more power there than just that of her sister.

"Where are Astra and Selene?" she asked. Maybe they were together, and they had done some pretty intense magic.

"They're safe with the alpha of another pack and his beta. They're probably a couple of hours from here."

Raven nodded. It couldn't be the twins, then. That hadn't been just a magic signature, that had been more magic than Raven had ever felt before.

"I don't like that I felt that and y—"

"Stop," Zane held out a hand to quiet her. Raven didn't like the way his entire demeanor had changed. Something was up. "Fuck. I think I hear the crunch of gravel on the road."

A deep cold sat at the bottom of Raven's stomach. She rushed to the cabin's front door and saw a car driving up the long driveway. The same car that had attacked them in front of Gemstones.

Oh, shit.

Oh, holy fuck.

"You were right," she whispered. "How could they have known I did magic?"

"I don't know," Zane grunted.

He stalked to the front door and poked his fingers through the blinds.

A million different questions swirled in Raven's head. How could the order have gotten to the cabin so fast? How was it possible that they were coming after her and not whoever had done that insane bit of magic?

"Fuck," he swore a blue streak and walked to a large cabinet in the living room. He pulled out two shotguns and some shells. "Do you know how to shoot?" he asked her.

Raven took a step back, gasping. "No, of course not."

"How much magic do you have left?"

She shook her head. "I don't know. Most of my typical supply. Putting up the wards wasn't that harrowing."

"Do you have enough to protect yourself? If they get me?"

"Get you?" The question came out like a panicked squeak.

"I don't know how many people are in that car, but they very well may overpower me. Then you'll have to defend yourself."

"Holy shit, what are you saying? You could die?" Panic made the bile in the back of the throat rise.

"I'm really hoping it doesn't come to that, but if it does…you use your magic as a last resort. Shoot first, okay? All you have to do is aim and be wary of the kickback. Don't put the gun inside of your shoulder, it could dislocate your arm. Got it?"

"No!" she screamed, not understanding every-thing that was happening in the moment. It was all too much.

"Hopefully, there aren't too many for me to deal with."

Zane peeked out of the window. "Fuck," he hissed.

"How many are there?" she whispered.

"Four. I think we might be outnumbered. How do the wards work? Can they get in?"

Raven nodded. "It protects against magic and unwanted energy. It also shields the cabin from tracking, but I guess that failed miserably the second I did magic to put them up in the first place."

"I'm going to shift and go out there. I'll try to do as much damage as I can. You call Betty, her number is in the phone." He pointed to where the silver device sat on the kitchen counter. "You tell her where we are and that we need backup."

"You're going out there?"

She knew he had to. It was that or wait for the members of the order to crash into the cabin. Zane didn't respond, but stripped quickly and shifted into his wolf. Raven opened the door for him to see four people climbing out of the car, loaded down by weapons.

Zane didn't waste any time. He launched

himself at the first person, a tall, wide man. Raven quickly shut the door and ran to the phone.

She pressed on Betty's number and walked back to the front door to see Zane snapping the neck of one of the attackers. The other three were circling him, guns at the ready.

"Zane's cabin. We're under attack," was all she said when whoever picked up.

She threw the phone down and cracked her fingers together. It was time to get her witch on. There was no way she was using the guns like Zane had instructed. She didn't know how her aim was, and she wasn't taking the chance to get Zane by accident.

She reached deep inside herself and called forth all of her magic. Remembering that last time, she had spent too much of her energy on making heavy airballs, she focused on making smaller ones that packed more of a punch. She opened the window off the living room, giving her the perfect vantage point to shoot airballs at the attackers. She trusted her aim more with her magic than with deadly bullets.

Taking a deep breath, Raven loosed one airball, and it met its mark, hitting one of the

Order members in the head. He was knocked down and out for a few seconds, but stood back up, shaking his head in confusion. He was looking around for her, she knew.

"The witch is here," he called out.

Raven ducked down just in time to see one of the attackers was Griggs, the man leading Salem's most deranged citizens on an odd crusade. She twirled her hands together and closed her eyes. She put in all of her fear and anger into three small airballs.

Squatting on her haunches, she peeked out of the window and blasted the three airballs at Griggs. Just in time, too, because his gun was pointing directly to Zane, who had another by the ankle. From her position in the cabin, Raven could see the bone protruding from the limb. That had to hurt like a motherfucker.

Was she having sympathy for that asshole? No. She shook the thought away. They were trying to kill her man. All to get to her.

With more speed and agility than she thought possible, she pelted tiny little airballs toward Griggs. A few of them landed squarely against his chest, others got him in the head. Furious, he pointed the gun in every direction.

"Where are you, you bitch?" he called out before laughing maniacally. "Gotta be in the cabin." He took a few steps toward the house, and Zane's neck snapped around.

Raven didn't want to let herself panic. She crouched and put her palms together. Between her hands, she created an airball. She spoke a protection spell over it, demanding that whatever higher power that had given her power protect her. With a deep breath, she crept up back to the window and threw her weapon directly at Griggs' heart.

The man was a couple yards outside from her hiding spot, a finger on the trigger already.

Everything happened at once.

The airball hit Griggs.

The gun went off, aimed directly at her. She realized her death was unstoppable. Except if...

Zane's wolf jumped in front of the bullet. The one that would have gotten Raven in the forehead had Zane not taken the hit.

A scream ripped out of her as Zane's body fell lifeless on the ground with a sad animal whimper.

Thankfully, Griggs was laid up by her airball. And two other order members were lying motionless on the ground. One of the two was groaning, surely due to his injured ankle.

The last psycho was pointing a gun at her through the window.

She ducked and army crawled to the front door. Could bullets pierce the cabin walls? That shit happened in movies, but could it happen in real life?

She made a few airballs and left them floating by her head before she swung the door open, still on the ground. A few shots fired above her head, no doubt because the bigoted idiot thought she would be standing.

Taking her chance, she threw the airballs, and as they flew, she made them as heavy as boulders. When they landed on the last members, the magic pinned him down as if he was imprisoned by invisible forces.

Raven ran to Zane, and her hand went to his wound. There was blood on his fur, but it was barely bleeding. The hole left by the bullet was somewhat closed.

She was about two seconds away from a full-blown panic attack when the red and blue lights of a police cruiser danced around the sky.

Help was there.

"Zane," she said, leaning her head down beside his head. "The humans are here, you have to shift back."

The wolf shook his head and huffed out air.

The police car came to a halt and two officers got out, guns drawn on her.

"I'm really sick of people pointing their guns at me," Raven said, putting her hands up. "I'll have you know, I'm the victim here."

"Raven?" one of the officers, a woman, asked.

"Yeah, Raven Bishop."

"I'm Betty."

"Shit, how did you get here so fast?! We're hours away from Salem."

"No, you're not. Zane drove you around for a long time to shake any tail. You're about ten minutes from the city limits."

"But we went to a small town…"

"Billings? That's a small fishing community up the river from the lake. Not well known except to fishermen. It was all an elaborate trick to make sure you didn't escape and get back to your sister."

"That jerk," she said, whirling back to Zane.

The wolf was no longer there.

"Where did he go?" she asked.

Betty cuffed the Order members while her partner did the same.

"Are you all right? You don't look injured." Betty's eyes surveyed her, and Raven shook her head.

"I'm fine. Zane?" she called out.

Her eyes fell onto Griggs. He wasn't moving, and his eyes were looking heavenward, wide open. Fear snapped inside her stomach and she had to swallow against the acid threatening to spew out.

"Is he…" her voice was barely audible.

"He's dead," Zane confirmed. He closed the distance between them. There was a small wound in his left shoulder, but he still wrapped Raven in his arms. "Are you okay?" he asked her.

"I'm fine. I'm exhausted, but I think I'm going to be all right. No obvious damage, but I think my magic is definitely depleted."

Zane ran his hands all over her body to confirm she was unharmed.

"Um, just so you know, you're still naked."

He looked down and shook his head. "I guess that's a trend between us."

"I don't like it," she grumbled.

"You don't?" He was genuinely surprised. "And here I thought you were into me."

"Well, of course, I am. I'm just not fond of the idea that my man's junk is out and about for everyone to see."

He chuckled, creating a grin. "Feeling possessive, are we?" he teased.

"No," she frowned. Then nodded her head. "Maybe. But you don't get the monopoly on possessiveness because you're the shifter. Witches are just as territorial, I'll have you know."

"It's fine, love," he said, kissing her softly. "You're okay," he repeated more for his benefit than hers.

"You tricked me. We're still technically in Salem."

"Yeah, sorry about that…"

"You're lucky I never leave my neighborhood, or I would have known."

"Okay, Sheriff, how are we playing this?"

"Call the coroner. Have him take Griggs' body. Call an ambulance and have the others on surveillance at the hospital. Some of the other Order members could try to bust them out. I'm going into my cabin and sleeping off this wound. Besides, Raven is about ready to pass out."

"No, I'm not." But she was. She hadn't realized she was completely leaning on Zane, or else she would have fallen over.

"Take care of this shit, Betty. I need to chill before I go out of my mind. I'll do all the paperwork in the morning."

"You got it, boss. I'll let Axel know not to disturb you until then. I'm going clothes shopping tonight." There was a smile on Betty's lips, one Raven didn't quite understand.

"Come on, Raven. Let's get you to bed."

And that was all she remembered before passing out in her man's arms.

EPILOGUE

RAVEN

Raven was vaguely aware she was lying on a cloud.

No, not a cloud. It was a bed, and a comfortable one. Why was there a heater beside her?

No, that was wrong, too. It wasn't a heater, it was a warm body. The body of her man.

"Zane," she cried out, sitting up.

"Wha—" he sat up, looking disoriented, his hair sticking up in a bunch of different directions. "What's wrong?" He pounced off the bed into a crouch, looking for a threat.

"What happened?" she asked, feeling like she had slept for years.

"Do you not remember?" he asked, rubbing a

hand over his face and then through his hair. "The fight with Griggs and then coming back into the cabin to get some rest?"

"Oh…" Pieces of the night were coming back to her. "I killed a man."

"It was killed or be killed, love," Zane said, gathering her up in his arms.

"But I didn't mean to," she said, feeling her heart break a bit.

"It was purely self-defense. You won't be charged. Not after all the evidence that was found against him and the Order of Salem."

"And Cerise? The twins? Where are they?"

"Everyone is fine, Raven. I'll explain everything to you as soon as you get up, shower, and eat. You've been asleep for a couple of days."

"What?" She pushed away from his embrace and moved away from the bed.

"You did a lot of magic. Remember?"

"Oh," that was right. "Bits are coming back… all of the airballs. Yeah."

Zane stood beside her. "When you weren't waking up, all I could do was lie beside you and sleep, so I didn't go crazy with concern."

"I'm fine. But you got shot."

"That healed almost the same day."

Raven ran her hand over where the shot had been. There wasn't even a scar.

"You're completely fine…" She was bemused.

"Not hardly." He kissed her. It was a rough kiss that didn't leave any place for breath. "I need to do this, okay?" he said. "I've been going out of my mind with worry."

He trailed kisses along her jaw before capturing her mouth in a desperate kiss. Raven wanted to push back against him, but it felt too good to be kissed by him. Like she had needed just that to really wake up from whatever slumber her magic had put her under.

Zane's hands went under her shirt, and then the garment was gone. Raven was a bit surprised to find she was now buck naked. He had clearly stripped her and put one of his own shirts on her so she could sleep in clean clothes.

His mouth closed on one of her nipples while his hand traveled down her stomach and cupped her pussy. One of his large fingers sought entrance, and Raven spread her legs a bit to let him in.

"This is going to be rough," he rasped in her ear. "I need to feel you."

"Then what are you waiting for?" she shot

back, desperately needing to be near him, too. She had almost lost him during the fight, and now she was done pretending he wasn't her man.

With a low, animal grunt, he lifted her clear off the floor and dropped her on the bed.

"Get on your hands and knees, love. I am going to take you. Hard and fast, but I'll make it good, baby."

He knelt behind her and pulled down his pajama pants. He stroked his cock while his other hand went to her clit. With able fingers, he twirled his digits around the hardened nub.

Raven didn't think she could climax so soon, so quick, so hard. But Zane knew just how to touch her. This was more than sex. It was a claiming, it was them coming together after almost losing the fight with the order.

"Are you ready for me, love?" he whispered in her ear.

"Fuck me," she purred.

And he did. With one smooth thrust, he seated himself completely inside her. Raven cried out, her pussy walls still clenching from the orgasm he had just given her.

Zane pumped in and out of her, saying her name over and over again. It was obvious this was a shifter thing. He had fought for her, now he needed to make sure she was there, that she was his.

Raven clamped down on his cock every time he reared in, desperate to come again, even if that made her greedy.

"Tell me you're mine forever, Raven."

"Forever," she agreed.

Raven felt the bite on the back of her neck, and it spurred on her orgasm. She came, fast and loud, Zane quickly falling into oblivion behind her. He kissed the mark, and then all the way down her spine and back up again.

"I'm going to love you and protect you until the day I die."

His vow was profound and resonated with her.

"Good," Raven purred, "because I'm in love with you in a pretty big way."

"I love you, too, my beautiful witch."

They snuggled on the bed together, Raven's head on Zane's shoulder while he danced his fingers up and down her back, occasionally getting all tangled up in her hair.

"So, I still don't know what happened with the order once Griggs died. And what about Cerise? How is she?" Raven asked.

"I'll let her tell you. She's got quite the tale to tell you."

"Zane Cross," she pinched his side, "I swear to god, you tell me right now…" The threat was weak, but hung in the air around them nonetheless.

"Well, it all started when she was doing a spell in the condo."

Zane wrapped her up in his arms and continued speaking, telling her impossible things.

One thing was certain, things had definitely changed for the Bishop women.

The End
….only not really… ;)
Not even by a little bit.

THE CASTERS & CLAWS SERIES

Spellbound in Salem

Seduced in Salem

Spellstruck in Salem

Surrendered in Salem

Get them all!

ABOUT THE AUTHOR

New York Times and USA Today Bestselling Author

Hi! I'm Milly Taiden. I love to write sexy stories featuring fun, sassy heroines with curves and growly alpha males with fur. My books are a great way to satisfy your craving for paranormal romance with action, humor, suspense and happily ever afters.

I live in Florida with my hubby, our kids, and our fur babies: Speedy, Stormy and Teddy. I have a serious addiction to chocolate and cake.

I love to meet new readers, so come sign up for my newsletter and check out my Facebook page. We always have lots of fun stuff going on there.

SIGN UP FOR MILLY'S NEWSLETTER FOR LATEST NEWS!

http://eepurl.com/pt9q1

Find out more about Milly here:
www.millytaiden.com
milly@millytaiden.com

ALSO BY MILLY TAIDEN

Find out more about Milly Taiden here:

Email: millytaiden@gmail.com

Website: http://www.millytaiden.com

Facebook: http://www.facebook.com/millytaidenpage

Twitter: https://www.twitter.com/millytaiden

ALSO BY MILLY TAIDEN

If you liked this story, you might also enjoy the following by Milly Taiden:

Sassy Mates / Sassy Ever After Series

Scent of a Mate *Book 1*

A Mate's Bite *Book 2*

Unexpectedly Mated *Book 3*

A Sassy Wedding *Short 3.7*

The Mate Challenge *Book 4*

Sassy in Diapers *Short 4.3*

Fighting for Her Mate *Book 5*

A Fang in the Sass *Book 6*

Also, check out the **Sassy Ever After World on Amazon or visit http://mtworldspress.com**

The Crystal Kingdom

Fae King *Book One*

Elf King *Book Two*

Dark King *Book Three*

Fire King *Book Four (TBA)*

Casters & Claws

Spellbound in Salem *Book One*

Seduced in Salem *Book Two*

Spellstruck in Salem *Book Three (TBA)*

Surrendered in Salem *Book Four (TBA)*

ALSO BY MILLY TAIDEN

Nightflame Dragons

Dragons' Jewel *Book One*

Dragons' Savior *Book Two*

Dragons' Bounty *Book Three*

Dragon's Prize *Book Four*

Wintervale Packs

Their Rising Sun *Book One*

Their Perfect Storm *Book Two*

Their Wild Sea *Book Three (TBA)*

A.L.F.A Series

Elemental Mating *Book One*

Mating Needs *Book Two*

Dangerous Mating *Book Three*

Fearless Mating *Book Four*

Savage Shifters

Savage Bite *Book One*

Savage Kiss *Book Two*

Savage Hunger *Book Three*

Savage Caress *Book Four*

ALSO BY MILLY TAIDEN

Drachen Mates

Bound in Flames *Book One*

Bound in Darkness *Book Two*

Bound in Eternity *Book Three*

Bound in Ashes *Book Four*

Federal Paranormal Unit

Wolf Protector *Federal Paranormal Unit Book One*

Dangerous Protector *Federal Paranormal Unit Book Two*

Unwanted Protector *Federal Paranormal Unit Book Three*

Deadly Protector *Federal Paranormal Unit Book Four*

Alpha Geek

Alpha Geek: *Knox*

Alpha Geek: *Zeke*

Alpha Geek: *Gray*

Alpha Geek: *Brent*

ALSO BY MILLY TAIDEN

Paranormal Dating Agency

Twice the Growl *Book One*

Geek Bearing Gifts *Book Two*

The Purrfect Match *Book Three*

Curves 'Em Right *Book Four*

Tall, Dark and Panther *Book Five*

The Alion King *Book Six*

There's Snow Escape *Book Seven*

Scaling Her Dragon *Book Eight*

In the Roar *Book Nine*

Scrooge Me Hard *Short One*

Bearfoot and Pregnant *Book Ten*

All Kitten Aside *Book Eleven*

Oh My Roared *Book Twelve*

Piece of Tail *Book Thirteen*

Kiss My Asteroid *Book Fourteen*

Scrooge Me Again *Short Two*

Born with a Silver Moon *Book Fifteen*

Sun in the Oven *Book Sixteen*

Between Ice and Frost *Book Seventeen*

Scrooge Me Again *Book Eighteen*

Winter Takes All *Book Nineteen*

You're Lion to Me *Book Twenty*

Lion on the Job *Book Twenty-One*

Beasts of Both Worlds *Book Twenty-Two*

Bear in Mind *Book Twenty-Three*

Come to Bear *Book Twenty-Four*

Wolfing Her Down *Book Twenty-Five*

Also, check out the **Paranormal Dating Agency World on Amazon**

Or visit http://mtworldspress.com

ALSO BY MILLY TAIDEN

Raging Falls

Miss Taken *Book One*

Miss Matched *Book Two*

Miss Behaved *Book Three*

Miss Behaved *Book Three*

Miss Mated *Book Four*

Miss Conceived *Book Five (Coming Soon)*

Alphas in Fur

Bears

Fur-Bidden *Book One*

Fur-Gotten *Book Two*

Fur-Given Book *Three*

Tigers

Stripe-Tease *Book Four*

Stripe-Search *Book Five*

Stripe-Club *Book Six*

Alien Warriors

The Alien Warrior's Woman *Book One*

The Alien's Rebel *Book Two*

ALSO BY MILLY TAIDEN

Night and Day Ink
Bitten by Night *Book One*
Seduced by Days *Book Two*
Mated by Night *Book Three*
Taken by Night *Book Four*
Dragon Baby *Book Five*

Shifters Undercover
Bearly in Control *Book One*
Fur Fox's Sake *Book Two*

Black Meadow Pack
Sharp Change *Black Meadows Pack Book One*
Caged Heat *Black Meadows Pack Book Two*

ALSO BY MILLY TAIDEN

Other Works

The Hunt

Wynters Captive

Every Witch Way

Hex and Sex Set

Alpha Owned

Match Made in Hell

Wolf Fever

ALSO BY MILLY TAIDEN

HOWLS Romances

The Wolf's Royal Baby

The Wolf's Bandit

Goldie and the Bears

Her Fairytale Wolf *Co-Written*

The Wolf's Dream Mate *Co-Written*

Her Winter Wolves *Co-Written*

The Alpha's Chase *Co-Written*

ALSO BY MILLY TAIDEN

Contemporary Works

Mr. Buff

Stranded Temptation

Lucky Chase

Their Second Chance

Club Duo Boxed Set

A Hero's Pride

A Hero Scarred

A Hero for Sale

Wounded Soldiers Set

If you enjoyed the book, please consider leaving a review, even if it's only a line or two; it would make all the difference and would be very much appreciated.

Thank you!

Made in the USA
Columbia, SC
25 July 2020